# *Martha's Journey*

## Renascence
## in a
## Mobile Home Park

*To Marilyn + Reed*
*My super Spanish*
*students & good*
*friends,*
*Peg Grimm*

*Peg Grimm*

First published by Dog Ear Publishing
4010 W. 86th Street, Ste H
Indianapolis, IN 46268
www.dogearpublishing.net

ISBN: 978-159858-659-6

This book is printed on acid-free paper.
This book is a work of Fiction. Places, events, and situations in this book are purely
Fictional and any resemblance to actual persons, living or dead, is coincidental.

Printed in the United States of America

# DEDICATION

The list could be longer than the pages of the book, and perhaps more interesting. To Pat Lawson who undertook the arduous task of reading my mangled hand writing and understanding my aged and garbled voice. Thank you so much.

To Carol Commodore who always encouraged me to write, who presented me with at least six empty notebooks in which I was to put down my weird and crazy thoughts. They are still empty, as are my thoughts.

To Susan Riley, the first person to read these words, and urged me to go on.

To Kath and Peggy, my loving daughters who care so much, who are so sensitive and tolerant of me and who are such amazing women. I am astounded at what they are and are still becoming.

To Annis Knakal, whose inspired artwork gave life and meaning to my words.

To the residents of my mobile home park who have provided me with the fodder and the foolishness, and the love. You have taught me a real sense of a caring community. I am grateful to you all.

Peg Grimm

## To the Reader (I hope there is at least one.):

When I was a junior in high school, I read Edna St. Vincent Millay's poem, *Renascence.* Her name fascinated me. Iambic pentameter. I really had a difficult time understanding what she was writing about. I wasn't smart or mature enough to get the gist of it—perhaps I still don't. It seems to me, however, that we are not re-born, but rather we assume new roles to play as we live out our lives. I was trying to articulate what happened in Martha's mind and soul as she overcame grief, anger, frustration, and loss. She had a new part to play in this stage of her life, and she played it with all her heart and played it well—not to applause, but to her own sense of being alive and vital.

Peg Grimm

# TABLE OF CONTENTS

# CHAPTER 1

# THE ARRIVAL

Pam noticed their car slowing down as they approached the entrance to Live Oaks Mobile Park.

"You having second thoughts, Mom?" she asked.

"Well, just a few I guess," was the reply. "This is a big step for me, you know."

"Of course, I know," Martha's daughter replied. "Oh, look, there's an old man on a three-wheeler bike waving at us."

"Oh, that's Ernie," her mother said. "He likes to greet everyone who arrives and direct them to their new unit. He's a bit over-friendly, but he means well and it gives him something to do. I met him last month when I checked out the place and again when I bought my new unit."

"Hi, Ernie. Remember me? I'm Martha Jenkins from Ohio."

"Oh, sure, I remember. You bought C52. Nice place. Needs a little work, but you'll love it. Who's that with you?"

"Ernie, meet my daughter, Pam. We can find our way, but thanks for greeting us. See you later."

And in this way, and at this moment, Martha Jenkins came to be a resident of Live Oaks Mobile Home Park.

Certainly a strange name for a park—Live Oaks Mobile Home Park, obviously nothing was mobile, or terribly much alive. These aluminum boxes, built in the years 1968-1973, were once on wheels and had been hauled down to south Florida from Indiana or Ohio or wherever. The wheels were mostly gone and the homes were placed on cement blocks <u>and</u> were skirted around the exterior with plastic trellis-like material.

There were two hundred and thirty-two units there. Some were single-wide with their original *salt map* style foam roofs; some were double-wide with roof overs. Most looked in pretty good shape—clean, neat, with orderly plantings, and many palm trees. There was a pond actually used for effluent from the septic tank. It was located in the middle of the park along with a recreation hall (also cement block), a pool, and the required shuffle board court. All in all it resembled any of the thousands of parks found throughout the state. They were a haven for fifty-five year olds and older, mostly middle class, mostly Middle Western, all retirees who wanted to escape the cold winters of the north and enjoy the affordable life style these parks offered.

# CHAPTER 2

## THE SEARCH

Martha's story mirrored many others. Her husband, Bill, had been a successful business rep, good income, nice home, two nice kids, a dog and a cat, and then at the age of sixty-three the dreaded "A" word, "Alzheimer's," hit. Martha gave up her job at the high school as an English teacher, and her life became an unending round of care and expenses beyond reasoning. Sadness was filling her days and nights, and hopelessness, her constant companion. Her solace was found in her faith, in the memories of their life before, and the love they shared. Her two kids, her four grandchildren, and her friends also provided solace, but not happiness.

Eventually the house had to be sold; the live-in care money dried up; the nursing home became her living space and then, he died. The end was almost anticlimactic. Day after day of seeing him, caring for him, watching him slip away, had totally consumed her every waking hour and lonely nights. And then it stopped. Her world stopped and suddenly she had to make decisions beyond spending eight hours visiting her non-responsive loved one, dragging herself home to a dead and quiet apartment and a sullen cat. The house was long gone, all her/their stuff sold, given away, trashed. There still were monstrous bills. She and her daughter and son and their families were totally exhausted, and now what?

He best friend, Beth, who had already traveled the rugged road map of widowhood, kept nagging her to get out, look around, find some open space, a new outlook. She should get out of the frozen, icy winters, look for the sun. She didn't say too much to her kids, just that she was going to look around. They had their own hills to climb; their own lives had hit the wall, too, and needed refocusing on the future.

So, off they went. Two sixty-six year old women feeling as if they were venturing into space without a space suit! The first stop was North Carolina. Beautiful, too cold. They had a few experiences in the restaurant with some old southern guys wanting to make these Yankee gals feel at home. It was almost laughable! Some good ole boys tried to pick them up in a Holiday Inn restaurant in Spartanburg, South Carolina. Then further south; again beautiful but cold. It was November. Charleston was intriguing, lovely, but a bit more costly than Martha wanted to consider. Beth was ready to decide on a place there, but they moved on. Georgia was okay, too. The lowland area south and east of Atlanta was fascinating, but, no, not that. Something was driving Martha, it seemed; but she truly didn't know what it was.

It didn't matter. They were having fun, being together, laughing and singing with the radio and avoiding "the end of the world sermons" found on the FM stations fading in and out. There certainly were a lot of those. Jacksonville was sort of scary because they got lost and had a hard time finding I-10. Martha had decided before they left that she would head southwest. Why? She wasn't at all certain.

At least it was getting warmer. They hit I-75 and headed south. Her original plan was to check out Sarasota, the Venice area, and then south.

Sarasota proved fascinating: The Ringling Estate, the Purple Von Wezel building, the Mote Lab, a beautiful water front. St. Armand's was to die for, but nothing clicked. Nobody had tried to pick them up since South Carolina. They decided that the number of women compared to the number of men in Florida made the chance of being hit on nearly an impossibility. No matter. That hadn't been the purpose of the trip, but the prospect wasn't totally unappealing.

By now they were pretty skilled at picking out motels and restaurants. They avoided the ones with the air conditioners in the room because they froze. They found Waffle Houses™ everywhere, and their AAA™ travel tick wasn't terribly accurate. They also realized that iced tea was always sweetened and grits came with eggs, no matter what!

They found some nice parks in the Venice area and were pleased with the city itself. But not exactly the spot Martha thought she was looking for. Onward they went, still enjoying each other's company. Still singing.

Beth was especially understanding of the moods that would overtake Martha: periods of silence, some tearful times, the need to be alone, the need to go to a movie, to laugh, to talk all night long. Later on, Martha would look back in wonder at the love and emotional support Beth had so freely given her.

# CHAPTER 3

# THE SEARCH CONTINUES

Next stop, Englewood; neither of them had ever heard of it. West of I-75 (old Tamiami Trail) then Route 776 ran through it, quite small actually, a bifurcated community, half in Sarasota County and half in Charlotte County. Martha sensed she might be getting closer or else perhaps she felt they were running out of time and energy. She instinctively knew that Beth would be returning north without making a commitment on a place here in Florida. She realized her friend was too well centered in her Ohio hometown. Too many connections to sever. Too content to leave. Unsure to start anew. Martha's last two years with Bill's illness had shut her off, had severed her connections and had made her convinced she would not rely on her kids to form her new life. She loved them with every inch of her being but she knew she had to begin her life in a new way or she would be forever broken, needy and an empty shell.

This insight was sensed by both of them and well understood. It only made them closer. Certainly by being true to their own personhood, would their friendship survive the trauma of whatever their future might hold? Aware of this, Martha discussed her plan to seek out a place in the Venice/Englewood area. Beth agreed enthusiastically as she knew where Martha was emotionally and recognized her friend's need to re-start her life. Perhaps the place wasn't the issue but rather the decision to choose a spot was truly the impetus for Martha's new voyage and new life.

So in agreement, in tandem, they set forth. There are hundreds of mobile home parks in that section of southwest Florida. Many are old, pretty ordinary. Some are newer manufactured homes, not mobile homes. Some are gated. And then that day they drove into Live Oaks Mobile Home Park. Beth questioned the name.

"Why Live Oaks, certainly they wouldn't call a place Dead Oaks Mobile Home Park, would they?"

Martha chuckled, "I'll have to ask the manager."

An old man on a three-wheeler bike approached.

"Hey ladies, I'm Ernie. I'm the official greeter. Are you looking to buy? I'll be happy to show you around."

"I'm Martha Jenkins and this is my friend, Beth. Could you point me to the manager's office please?"

"Of course," came the reply. And the old guy saluted. "I see you have Ohio plates, quite a few from Ohio here. Follow me." And that's how it all began.

# CHAPTER 4

## DAY ONE—OPENING THE DOOR

Now, months later, Martha and her daughter, Pam, had returned and were slowly following Ernie who was pumping furiously on his old three-wheeler bike. They stopped at the manager's office and Paul Tyler stepped out to greet them holding a clip board and dangling a set of keys in the other. Behind him was his wife, Betty.

"Welcome to Live Oaks," they said in near unison. "We were expecting you."

Martha opened the door of her car, stepped out and shook Paul's hand and his wife hugged her saying welcome again. Martha introduced her daughter, Pam, and then went into the small office to fill out yet more papers. Paul mentioned to Ernie that he could head back to the park entrance as more people were due the same day. With some reluctance Ernie took his leave, saluted, and pedaled off.

The office smelled as if cookies might be baking in the kitchen and Betty soon reappeared with a plat of ginger snaps and iced tea (sweetened, of course!). They chatted a while about the weather in Ohio, cold, icy, snowy. Martha was truly anxious to get to her place. She knew her time with Pam was limited. Pam recognized her mother's mood and suggested they might want to hurry on and get settled. The manager and his wife got the idea pretty quickly. They were just trying to be friendly and solicitous as they both knew this was a new and unknown experience for Martha and her daughter. They had been through this initial house opening with many others. It was an emotional experience. Most people took it all in stride and adapted quickly while others never really crossed the threshold and remained unhappy people or left soon after. Paul and Betty hoped Martha would have a positive response to her new life as they both thought she was a quality person and they had enjoyed her friend Beth on the initial meeting months ago.

Paul chuckled to himself remembering old Leo's reaction to Beth. Of course, Leo hit on all the new women who arrived, desperately hoping he'd find someone capable of mowing his lawn, picking up his socks, baking a home-made lemon pie, oh, and cleaning his fish. So far he hadn't found anyone who fit the bill, or anyone who was willing. Paul knew there were quite a few Leos in the park, lonely old men looking for a woman to fill the empty space in their hearts and homes. Just as there were certainly more countless women looking for such a man, someone to hug, to laugh with, to fuss over, just to fill the awesome loneliness they lived with. It was all so sad. He honestly believed the park presented the best possible opportunity to lessen the situation, the awful emptiness. He wasn't involved with matchmaking, but he felt this place offered many the opportunity to have a more fulfilling life. He wanted to do all that he and his wife could to help Martha. He thanked God again and again for the commitment of his wife Betty after many miserable years of his being alone. So, he wished this new resident the best with all his heart and directed her and her daughter to their new beginning.

# CHAPTER 5

## WALKING IN

Walking in, Martha had forgotten much of what she'd seen before. Then she had been focused on the decision, not the surroundings. Foolishly perhaps, but that was then and now was now. She noticed Pam stop a bit and look around before she stepped over the two and an half steps into her mom's new space.

"Well, it's bright and cherry, isn't it?" Pam knew she was a bit startled, and sensed her mother knew what she was thinking. Their family home had been large and spacious and warm. Her mom's apartment had been smaller, but also a warm space. Though empty, this was pretty sterile and pretty small.

Well, it won't take a lot of energy to keep this place clean and sparkling, will it?" she enthused.

"You don't have to pretend, Pam! It's not Ohio anymore." Martha hugged her daughter, wiped away a small tear, waved good-bye, and said thanks to Paul and Betty who had brought the plate of cookies in to them. She closed the door and said with a huge breath of false exhilaration, "All right, let's get to it."

And together mom and daughter began to unpack. Pam had a hidden bouquet of flowers she had picked up at Wal-Mart and put them in a cracked glass in the center of the dinette table. It was a bright moment in a rather dreary day.

"Hey, Mom, how come the bathroom floor is sorta like a trampoline?"

"Don't know, didn't notice that! We'll check it out later."

"Oh, the toilet doesn't flush!" again from the bathroom.

"Maybe the water valve's turned off."

"What valve? Don't see any."

"Oh, well, that's another thing to check out."

"Did you turn on the air conditioner?"

"No, I'll do it."

A short time later a terrific loud BANG! Sparks, fire outside the bedroom window.

"Holy Cats!! What was that?" yelled Pam.

"I don't know; we better check it out."

"I'll check it out now, call 911."

"The phone's not hooked up yet."

"I'll use my cell."

"I'll call the manager."

"Oh, he's here already. He must have been nearby."

"Where's your circuit breaker box, Martha?"

"I didn't even know we had one."

"I'll find it," shouted Pam. "There, I turned them all to off. What happened?"

"Guess the AC blew up," muttered Paul.

"Wow, what a beginning!"

"I heard you say something about the toilet?"

"Toilet's inoperable," whispered Martha.

"Ya got that right, Mom. Oh well, we'll figure it out. Let's go have dinner, go to bed, get a good night's sleep, and tackle all this tomorrow."

"Good idea!" from Paul. "I'll get the AC man out here and I can check out the plumbing tomorrow. Tomorrow will be a better day."

"God, I sure hope so," echoed from both Martha and Pam in unison.

"Oh, my lord!" yelled Paul. "Here comes Ernie pedaling away! He's a retired fire fighter. Better take cover. He's lugging two huge fire extinguishers."

"Hey, Ernie, it's okay. Fire is mostly out; you can head on back to the entrance."

"No siree, Paul. These ladies need protection." And with that he proceeded to spray his fire extinguisher all over the air conditioner, which was still smoldering, as well as the plants, the side of the mobile, and himself. Martha and Pam crouched down in amazement.

"Ernie! Enough, enough!" Paul ran out to grab the second extinguisher. "Thanks a lot, but we're okay here. Good job. Thanks, okay now."

Martha and Pam at first had glazed expressions, then Pam burst out into fits of laughter, and Paul heaved a sigh of relief. Martha's Day One was almost over!

More to come……….

Before departing for dinner, Pam flipped the circuit breakers so there would be electricity for the water heater, the lamps, and the stove.

That night is etched in Pam's mind forever as the "Night of the No -See-Ums." Returning full, sated, and tired from a very good meal of fish chowder and grouper at Barnacle Bailey's, Martha and Pam trooped into the mobile home and got ready for bed. Paul had fixed the commode so it worked; the shower worked; the floor was still wavy, but Pam thought it might have been the mojitos; and now, as in *Pepy's Diary,* 'And so to bed.'

There were two bedrooms, one very tiny and one good sized. Pam chose the tiny room thinking her mom might want to be alone, and besides, she had a book she was into and wanted to read a little. No air conditioning, so the windows were open. She had checked for screens; she thought all was in order. Wrong! Within twenty minutes she started itching—her neck, arms, feet sticking out from the sheets. The itching got worse. She got up and checked the places that itched but didn't see any bugs, though she did see pink welts. They itched and itched hellishly! Her mom heard her moving around in the tiny bedroom and called out.

"What's the matter?"

Pam told her about the itching and her mom replied, "Oh, Pam, I forgot to tell you; those are no- see- ums."

"They're what?"

"The tiny bugs you can't see that come in through the screen when the lights are on."

"No- see- ums?"

"Yes, I have some ammonia in the bathroom; rub it on, and turn off your light. I'm terribly sorry. Good night, again."

Finally, the end of Day One in Live Oaks Mobile Home Park.

# CHAPTER 6

## DAY TWO

---

Pam awoke around 6:30 AM still itching to find her Mom sitting in a chair in the small living room paging through a photo album they had brought in the night before. The smell of coffee had awakened her.

"Tough night, Mom?"

"A little. I was too tired to have a really bad time. I slept pretty well. I just don't know what to start first and my time with you is too precious to waste on mundane things."

Don't worry, Mom; I'll be back. Let's have some breakfast and start a list. You're the best list writer I've ever known. Let's have English muffins, cream cheese and orange marmalade."

"Good idea. We'll use the oven as the toaster doesn't work. As far as lists are concerned, I always write them and then I always forget where I put them."

"I know, but it'll put our thoughts in order. OK, I'll fix the muffins; you write."

"Well, number one, the AC has to be fixed or replaced. Paul said he'd tend to that. Number two, we've got to check out the floor in the bathroom and I can't stand the carpeting in the living room. It's that mustard-colored shag and it's truly awful. I didn't notice it last time I was here. They must have spilled a lot of stuff on it."

"You noticed! OK. Step two, a carpet/flooring store and step three, I really think you need to have all the

plumbing checked out. It looks like the hot water heater—
that tiny thing under the kitchen sink—leaks, or something
does; and the floor is a little wavy here too. And it isn't cuz
of the drinks we had last night."

"You're right. I noticed that too! Oh, Pam, I forgot
to thank you for the bouquet. It looks lovely there, cracked
glass and all."

"Well, it's no wonder you forgot. It's not every day
you have an air conditioner blow up and an ex-firefighter
maniac spray stuff all over hell and everyone. Wow! What
a day!"

"Well, it's a bit hilarious in retrospect."

"I'm glad you can laugh about it, Mom."

# CHAPTER 7

## SHOPPING

They finished breakfast. The kitchen got pretty hot from the oven so off they went stopping at the manger's office to see if he'd found the AC man, and if he could recommend a plumber. Pam had her own list of some colorful towels, sheets, placemats, and furniture covers to brighten up the surroundings. She also wanted to bring back some fresh shrimp, veggies, and fruit. The refrigerator seemed to function OK, so that was a relief.

They headed toward Port Charlotte, a new area for them. On the way, they passed through a little burg called El Jobean. "What a strange name", Pam thought. She wondered if they called it "El Hobean," like in Jose. Martha didn't know either. Port Charlotte, south toward Punta Gorda, turned out to be a rather strange city. Along Highway 41, Tamiami Trail, there was one very large mall with all the usual big stores; then strip malls one after the other on both sides, all the way to the Peace River Bridge. There were fast food places, stores of every description, bars, pawn shops, tattoo parlors, more shops, on and on.

Martha was looking for a certain carpet store on the left or south side of 41 and Pam was planning on hitting Macy's™ at the mall on their return. They found the carpet store nestled between a weight loss place and a German butcher shop—a really eclectic area.

The carpet store was bright and cheery with loud music bouncing off the walls. A sharply dressed middle-aged man with a New Jersey accent latched on to them, ushering them here and there and talking a mile a minute. Pam noticed her mother's edginess and grabbed the man by the arm and suggested he slow down and not talk so loudly. Keeping his arms from failing about would have been a good idea, but she thought she'd skip that suggestion for now.

Pam had the measurements of the living room and the main bedroom, and Martha had decided on a tan color and a tight weave, non-wool. They found a roll of carpeting that seemed to fit, and Pam thought the price of $10.95 a yard installed with pad sounded right. Then Martha found a soft teal for the bedroom, same type of carpet. So the deal was set and as today was Tuesday, they were to install both pieces on Friday sometime in the morning. Pam had them agree to haul out and get rid of the old carpeting and pads. It appeared that all was taken care of and her mom was happy. Step two was a done deal, she thought.

Then on to the mall. Pam found some bright and cheery placemats and towels for the kitchen, both at Macy's™. She also talked her mom into buying a new swimming suit for the pool and a book at Barnes and Nobel™ on Mobile Park living. Then on to lunch at "Red Lobster™;" a stop at "Sam's™" for the basics, a toaster; and then home. On arriving back to their mobile home, they found Ernie hosing off the AC, the plants, and the wall, and singing happily to himself. Pam thought he might turn out to be a little too much, but Martha was okay with it. So nothing was said except "thanks."

Next stop, the pool. Pretty small by resort standards, but clean and inviting. They showered at the solar shower on the deck and paddled about for an hour or so. There was one other woman in the pool and she swam laps furiously, counting them off as she touched the end. At one hundred and thirty-two she stopped, said hello, climbed out of the pool, said good-bye, and left! Well, that was not too friendly, thought Pam. Oh well, back to fix dinner and check to see if the TV was functioning.

They found a note fixed to the front door from Paul, the manager. The AC man had stopped by and the bad news was that it was beyond repair. The good news was the repair guy had a last year's model in hand and could install it Thursday for $3250. Martha thought she'd better go ahead, so she called and set up the appointment. Item one now was checked off. Things were moving forward. Next on the list, the plumber.

Pam boiled some fresh shrimp, made a green salad, sliced tomatoes and put out the hard rolls she picked up. The key lime pie would finish off dinner in great style. The placemats and napkins were a great addition, and the Pinot Grigio added a festive note! Day two seemed to have gone pretty well, and Martha looked rather content—not terribly joyous, but content. They didn't put the lights on, but the new candles cast enough light. The TV was working but the number of channels seemed pretty limited. They settled for "Dancing with the Stars." Pam suggested a short walk before retiring and off they went.

It was rather eerie walking around the park at night. There were street lights, of course, so it wasn't truly dark and the moon was shining. Pam noticed all the strange items in the planters and near the front doors. There were collections of ceramic cats at one place, turtles at another. One unit had ceramic elephants of all sizes. There were old snow shovels labeled "gone to rest." Silhouettes of large "behinded" women peeking behind a tree—what was that all about? Generally, however, the planters were well cared for, not too many gee jaws, and then there were many tall palms. Bougainvillea and the hibiscus plants were beautiful and flourishing. They stopped at the laundry and checked it out. Modern appliances and neat as a pin. A lost black sock hung from a short clothes bar. Martha realized single socks were a phenomenon even here. They popped into the recreation hall and noticed the book cases, ping pong table, and exercise equipment in the pool/billiard room. Nobody was about, but by now it was near 9:00 PM and all was quiet. Back home again, Pam wished she could read but was content to sit in the lanai and think about what they had accomplished. The plumbing would be next and she thought she'd buy her mom a bike.

Pam's bites were still bothersome, but she went to bed and fell asleep pretty quickly. She thought before dropping off, of the changes occurring in her mother's life and how she would return to her husband, kids, and job in

Ohio. Her mom would begin a new life without any of those supports. Sometimes lately when she saw old couples walking hand in hand, she felt anger at the unfairness of it all. It was beyond understanding. She knew her mother was doing everything in her power to be independent and not lean on her kids. She loved and respected her for that desire, but it hurt. She missed her dad like crazy. She thought she had dealt with her anger and loss, but at this moment she realized she had not. Oh well, it was her mother's needs right now. She'd deal with her problem later. And so to sleep.

# CHAPTER 8

## DAY THREE

---

Awakened at 6:00 AM or so to the smell of coffee and the sound of a newspaper page turning, Pam made her way to the living room. Her mother was sitting with a cup of coffee in one hand and the paper in the other. Martha looked up smiling and wished her good morning.

"Good morning to you, Mom. How did last night go? No bugs for me. That bug spray from Sam's™ seemed to work."

"Fine, Pam. The bed is quite comfortable. I'd rather trade it in for a queen size. I don't need a king size, so that could be another item for the list. Maybe before the carpet gets here."

"Good idea, Mom. Coffee smells good. Can I refill yours?"

"Yes, please. Been reading the paper. It's strange to read about places I never heard of. Weather's supposed to be good for the rest of the week. We should plan something fun. I'd like to take you to the Ringling Home and St. Armand's Circle."

"Sure, let's get our stuff done here and then let's play. We need to get a plumber in here. We'll get a name from Paul and Betty this morning."

They were startled by a loud knock on the door. Pam went to the door and opened it to find a middle-aged man with a huge mustache facing her.

"Mrs. Jenkins?"

"No, I'm her daughter.  Who are you?"

"I'm the guy from the carpet store.  We wanted to check out the site before we hauled the carpeting here." All of this was said slowing in what sounded like a heavy Slavic accent.

"Ok," said Pam.  Let's see your order form."

"Right here, lady.  See dar it is!"

The big guy tramped in followed by a little guy with an equally huge mustache.  He didn't say a word.

"Ya see we have to check the under layment.  Dese old places have particle board under neat da rugs and if it gets wet it swell up—that's why your kitchen floor is like da ocean; please let me move da couch."

He and his helper pulled out the couch and began to pull up an edge of the carpeting.  After several minutes of pulling, it broke loose and the smaller guy walked over and fell through the floor!

"Holy shit!" he yelled.

Martha and Pam both jumped up and ran over behind the couch.  The poor guy had both legs stuck in the hole and was at least three feet down.

"I sue; I break my leg!  I mad as hell!"

"Oh, my gosh!" this from Pam and Martha.

"This bad, very bad!" yelled the big man.  "He sue for sure."

Pam dragged out her cell phone and dialed the manager.  "Poor guy, we're wearing him out," she thought.

They all stood looking at each other, nobody saying anything.  The big guy kept repeating, "He right, he sue, maybe he break leg."

"Well," yelled Pam, "why don't you help him out of the hole? He can't stay there."

By the time they got the smaller guy out of the hole, Paul had arrived.

"Oh, it's you guys. What are you two doing here? Didn't I kick you out last week?"

"We come to check out the chob."

"Oh no, you don't. You came to get a job to replace the under layment and they aren't going to hire you two blokes! Out a here now!"

At this point the two slink away and out the door, muttering.

"Sorry this happened," said Paul. "You may have to get some reputable people to check the under layment. These guys are crooks and illegals as well."

"Well, thanks for coming again, Paul," said Martha. "I'll call the store and figure out what's going on. If we have to put in some new plywood, then we will. Mobile homes are certainly different. I didn't realize all the complications."

"Well, not everyone has an AC blow up and some unscrupulous yokel fall through the floor. Don't worry; it will get better. Trust me."

"I hope so," from Martha and Pam. "Now, what about a plumber?"

"Stop by and I'll give you a few names. One is a retired guy in the park and one has his own business in Englewood. They're both used to dealing with mobile home plumbing. As you've probably guessed, everything is smaller and I'm sad to say, more cheaply made. So problems arise. Once you get on top of these problems largely due to lack of use, you'll be fine. Remember, this place was open for a year. So, take heart!"

"I sure hope so, and I'll take heart. I'm a positive person," said Martha.

"You've got that right! Mom."

"I thought so," said Paul.

# CHAPTER 9

## NEW NEIGHBOR

Then a knock at the door. Pam answered and an elderly, little lady stood there with a plate of baked goods of some sort.

"Come in," said Pam. "Sure smells great! I'm Pam, and this is my mom, Martha. Of course, you know Mr. Tyler."

"Good morning, all of you. I'm Mabel Johnson and these are some of my scones. I wanted to welcome you as soon as I could and tell you how happy I am to have somebody living next door. Oh, and here's our park paper, *The Monthly Muse*. You're in it as a 'New Comer' – so welcome, and I hope we'll get to be good friends. Do you play euchre or canasta? We need players, and shuffleboard is Saturday morning. And there's a Ladies Club meeting Monday morning. Oh, it's all in the paper. Nice meeting you, and welcome again. Bye for now."

"Good-bye, Mabel and thanks. These scones look wonderful, and we'll certainly enjoy them." Martha took Mabel's hand and led her to the door.

"Whew! What a morning!" exclaimed Pam.

"Yes, I agree," from Paul Tyler. "I'll be getting back. Betty will think I fell in the pond or something else blew up. See you later with the plumbers' names. Bye."

"Bye."

"Bye. Wonder if every day's going to be like this?"

"I don't know, Pam. We can only hope it will get better," said her mom. "Well, where were we? Oh, yes, let's eat a scone, and I'll call the carpet guy and try and get this straightened out. Then the plumber. Then, let's drive to Sarasota, have lunch at the Columbia at St. Armand's. I need to get away a little, I think."

"Great idea! Mom. Oh, these are really good."

So they made the calls, went through the Ringling Estate, and had a wonderful lunch at the Columbia Restaurant in St. Armand's Square. Pam was truly impressed, and stuffed. They looked at some great shops, didn't buy anything, but had fun. Home again, a brief swim, grouper for dinner, candles and wine, some TV, and off to bed. Tomorrow the rugs would be down, AC the next day, plumber coming Saturday. Imagine, on Saturday, and no time and a half!

# CHAPTER 10

# DAYS FOLLOW

Time was flying by and Pam would be leaving Monday. Martha would drive her to Sarasota for her flight back to Ohio. She was already dreading that goodbye, but knew she had to get past this in order to move forward. How lucky she was to have Pam as a daughter. She was already looking forward to next month when Bill, Jr. would be down for a few days with Elaine and the kids. She would have a honey-do list for him as she used to have for his dad. "Used to", that was long ago, and the thought hurt. Oh, well, time to move on. Say a little prayer, and move onward, onward.

The days moved on. The carpet was laid; some under layment had to be replaced, but not a significant amount. They decided to wait on the queen size bed. Bill, Jr., his wife and kids would enjoy the king size bed. Another swim, went to Publix™, picked up some chicken breasts, rice, broccoli, more salad greens, Riesling wine, and some *Cherry Garcia*™ ice cream—heavenly. The air conditioner was installed and worked great. Pam could read at night with the air on and the windows closed.

The plumber replaced some parts of the commode and checked all the faucets and drains. A new shower part was needed, and he suggested Martha replace the water heater. It was a 1968 model and certainly had had a long life. So things were shaping up. Pam bought Martha a used bike, borrowed one from a neighbor, and the two tooled around the park and nearby area. They went to the beach, taking a picnic lunch, swam in the pool, and walked the park, meeting and greeting the local residents. Most all seemed friendly and generally pleased to see them, Mabel and Ernie most of all. Sunday they visited a local church and felt truly welcome.

Monday came and the trip to Sarasota airport. She hated to see her daughter go, but she wasn't as torn as she thought she might be. Coming back and walking into her place alone was a bit off putting—which is a nice way of saying "not good"—but she found a note Pam had left behind on the table

*Dear Mom, you dear and special person you,*

*You are stronger than you can ever imagine. The last years, the terribly tough years, have shown you to be a tower of strength, of caring, of meeting everything head on with determination and humor. Bill, Jr. and I are so proud of you, more than you could ever imagine. You're on your way, Mom; go for it! You've earned it; we're behind you.*

*With love, your favorite daughter, P.*

*P. S. We're only a few hours away. You have need—we're there!*

Reading the note, she recognized in her daughter's words that it was time to get on with her life.

# CHAPTER 11

## MORE REPAIRS

---

She found a guy in the park who replaced the linoleum in her kitchen and bathroom floors, and obviously placed some new plywood underneath. Things were moving along. Some vertical blinds were due the end of the week. She had picked up an old portable Singer sewing machine at the Goodwill™ and was working on new covers for the cushions on the lanai. Before Pam left she had purchased two hibiscus plants, a red and a violet bougainvillea. Things were a changing.

So, life went on. Six weeks later, her son and family came for six days, and she was ecstatic. He built her a planter, trimmed bushes and trees, made order of chaos in the shed. He complimented her on her progress and told her he was proud of her for all she had done, and all she was doing now. She was deeply touched.

The manager and his wife continued to be helpful and friendly. She had a few small dinner parties for neighbor friends she had made. Simple dinners and nice conversation. And everyone left by 9:00 PM. Ernie was still Ernie; Mabel kept making scones. It had become a peaceful and reasonable lifestyle. She was looking forward to Beth's arrival. She felt the need for girl talk, silliness, and fun. Guess she'd never get over that.

Pam and the kids would be there for spring break. Maybe they'd go to Disney World™, maybe not. See what they really wanted to do. The beach was lovely, and handy.

The pool was great. She'd borrow a few bikes and they'd plan a picnic to a nearby island. Maybe she'd rent a pontoon boat and they'd go fishing and visit yet another island. So much to do, so little time.

It seemed ages since the air conditioner blew up, Ernie sprayed the extinguisher, and one guy fell through the floor. The carpeting was beautiful and easy to care for. The toilet worked, the floors were no longer wavy, and the flowers were blooming. Life was good and things were all right in her world—or as right as they could be. Would she ever get over missing him? No, of course not. But she had to admit that living in this mobile home park was the closest thing she could find to living a happy and fulfilled life. There was a real sense of community here. There were caring people living here who did not hide their caring hearts.

# CHAPTER 12

## GATORS, IGUANAS, AND OTHER CRITTERS

Martha had noticed a gator or two swimming in the pond. The large brow and eyes appearing above the surface of the water was ample evidence of their presence. That was as close as she wanted to be to these strange prehistoric-like creatures. Her neighbor, Mabel, a font of park lore, told her a story that was at once frightening and hilarious.

Jackie, a resident of F row, was backing her car out of her carport. She looked in her rear view mirror, then left, and right, and then glanced ahead. There on the floor of her carport was what she assumed to be a blown-up gator kid's pool toy. She stopped the car, got out and was going to pick it up, when the thing moved and its jaw opened wide! She thought it was a prank played by her neighbor, Wilfred, until she saw the rows of huge white teeth and the moving tail! Scared out of her wits, she stepped back and fell into her bougainvillea bush, yelling her lungs out as she fell.

Wilfred heard her screams and rushed over. He had been sweeping his carport with a broom. Without thinking, he stabbed at the gator with his broom. The animal grabbed the straw end of the broom in its jaws and started swinging it around. Wilfred jumped back in panic and then saw Jackie flailing away in the flower bush. Bougainvilleas have thorns and she was bleeding all over. The gator had quieted down a bit so Wilfred helped Jackie to her feet and took her over to his unit. His wife, Nora, would clean her up and put on some band-aids while he called the Department of Natural Resources (DNR). People were milling about but nobody came very close. Gators were prevalent in Florida but this was the first one anybody had seen lying in a carport.

Then, wonder of wonders. That very night, Jackie's neighbor, Marie, in the unit behind on E Street, awoke in the night. She needed to visit the "facilities" as she usually did around 3 AM. She turned on the light, lifted the lid of the commode, and screamed bloody murder! Nestled under the lid was a three and one-half foot iguana! Marie was so frightened; she had an accident, which only made the situation worse. She probably should have sat down, but she was too scared to move. Someone was pounding on her door, as her screams had awakened at least eight people from a deep sleep. She insisted she had to get ready before she'd let anyone in. She went to Mabel's house to sleep that night. The DNR was called again. It was a long time before Marie felt comfortable getting up at night. She borrowed a portable commode from the American Legion. That event entered the rolls of park history as the "Fright of the Iguana!"

Another critter story was related to Martha. This concerned armadillos. These irksome animals chewed up the lawns searching for grubs. After an armadillo attack, the yards looked like the pitching area of a golf course. One park resident sought help from the "True Value" man. He suggested putting moth balls in the entrance of the armadillo's lair below the mobile home while boarding up the exit opening. Wilfred, who had jousted with the gator, bought the mothballs. They were thrown in as directed. The next morning, when his wife looked out the window she yelled,

"Will, come here! You won't believe it!"

"What?" came from the living room.

"It must have hailed last night."

"It doesn't hail in this part of Florida."

"Well, come here and look!"

And sure enough, according to the storyteller, the moth balls were all over the side lawn. On further inspection, they discovered marks of the animal's tail as he or she swept the moth balls out of the lair. Armadillos are pretty clever critters.

Other stories concerned palmetto bugs, a high-class name for cockroaches. They truly are everywhere. What can be worse then getting up in the middle of the night, padding in bare feet to the bathroom, and stepping on a three and one-half inch bug? Not a pleasant thing to do. On the flip side, there are geckos. These are rather fun. They are curious creatures and will watch you and appear very friendly. Of course, when you move, they run away like greased lightening. Martha enjoyed them as long as they stayed out of her kitchen. She now realized that animals and fish and bugs were all a part of the Florida landscape.

# CHAPTER 13

## BOOSTER MEETINGS

---

Of course there are the Booster Meetings! The second Tuesday of every month, the Boosters (the parks social planning group) have a meeting. Coffee and donuts are served free (donation suggested); annual dues, $5.00 per person. Meetings are run according to *Robert's Rules of Order.* Very few know who "Robert" is! They have motions, and seconds and discussions, although more often than not, someone hollers out, "Hell, why are we discussing anything? Let's vote; we already have motions, seconds. This is a waste of time." There's a lot of "ya, ya's; let's vote" and away it goes. It is sort of a fun time.

Then someone would bring up an idea.

"I make a motion we go over to the golf course down the road and demand they give us tee times every Friday morning at 9:00 AM. Any second?"

"I second the motion. I love to play golf!" And away they would go. The president would interrupt and kindly tell the guy the motion was not on the agenda. That if he presented it to a board member prior to the next meeting, it could be placed on the agenda. He also would inform the individual making the motion that the golf course was a private course and wouldn't allow non-members to play. But the motion maker was not dissuaded and kept going on and on. Then announcements are made about coming events and it's amazing the number of activities people could be involved in—fun things, learning things, helping things.  Martha felt proud on hearing all these presentations.

Committees. Martha was surprised at the emphasis in forming committees in the park.  Mabel had talked her into signing up to help for the next week's "Chili Colossal." The following Wednesday afternoon, eight home owners assembled in the Recreation Hall.  Sue Longwood was in charge, it seemed, but not for long.  George spoke up immediately and insisted he would be the chief cook, as he had filled that position for ten years.  A new member shyly asked what recipe he was using.

"My own," he replied.

"Well, I'd like to hear how you do it."

"I use ground beef, canned tomatoes, onion, chili powder, ya know, the usual."

"Ground beef?"

"Of course, what would you use, ground elk?"

"No, of course not.  I use ground turkey!"

And off it went.  The ground beef only folks calling the ground turkey people, "pansies, food faddists, wimps, etc."  It got a little noisy and certainly was out of hand.  It was the men who were arguing.

Sue, a large woman, and a former high school principal, stood up and shouted,

"Boys, that's enough!  Shut up and sit down."

"But, Sue...."

"Enough I said.  This year we'll try fifty percent beef and fifty percent turkey.  Now, let's get on with it."

A meek voice from the smallest person in the group, "Do you use carrots?"

"Carrots?" from several speakers.

"Yes, you need carrots to off set the tomato acid, and…."

"Off set what? Oh, for heavens sake! This is getting ridiculous."

Sue stood up again and said, "The chief chef will use his recipe with the compromise on ground turkey. Let's move on!"

The meeting dragged on with fights over the garlic bread—pre-garlic butter or add it later. It was truly comical and afterward Martha remarked to Mabel that a committee was certainly a concoction designed by a double-humped camel. It was a memorable time, however, and she sensed there were many more of these meetings to come. As time went on, Martha and Mabel would whisper "turkey" and the other would respond "carrots" when meetings of whatever kind went out of control, and that was more than a "sometime thing."

# CHAPTER 14

## POT-LUCKS

There are a million things to learn in a mobile home park! Number one, Martha found out, was understand the principle of the "Pot-Luck" get-togethers. The protocol was more Byzantine than the worst of the Tsarist regime.

One row in the park was in charge each month and the oldest people in the row were really in charge—and you better believe it! You must do everything precisely the way you have done it since 1972 or else. So Martha volunteered as it was her row that had this month's pot-luck. She asked what she could do and was told to help with the table setting—napkins, salt, peppers, creamer, sugars, and water pitchers. But it had to be two creamers, two sugars per table— not three, no, never three. She found that out in a hurry! People brought their own silverware, and plates, wine or soda, and a dish to pass. The residents also learned what dishes to look for and hid them behind the piano. That was the reason to be the month's hostess—you had first dibs! So Martha was finding her way, meeting some very nice people, beginning to feel like she really belonged. She missed her best friend, Beth; missed the all-night talks, the okay to cry; missed Pam, Bill, Jr., her grandkids. MISSED BILL!

She enjoyed the pot-luck, the singing afterward, the clean up. She recognized in the glances and overt looks, the hurting eyes of many women her age. She would seek them out. She also signed up for shuffle -board and golf—

why not? She hadn't had a golf club in her hand in more than three years. Maybe this was the chance to give it a try again. Now shuffle -board did not have the same appeal, but she'd try it. Bingo—no, not yet. She wasn't ready, although she realized it was popular here. Yoga, bridge, those two were more intriguing here. So day-by-day, she became more involved.

# CHAPTER 15

# JIMMY BUFFET

One of the high lights of the season was the Jimmy Buffet night. The Rec Hall was decorated to resemble a tropical paradise. Carpet rolls were painted and palmetto fronds stuck in the cylinders, and they did look like palm trees. There was a palmetto- covered entrance, Tiki lamps, and the walls and tables were decorated with all manner of stuff. People wore Hawaiian shirts, straw hats, and shell necklaces. The women who decorated the hall were experts. The hall was truly transformed.

There was a band. A live band, and it was good. People brought their own liquid refreshments, and were quite sufficiently prepared. Everybody danced. So many, it was almost butt-to-butt, but nobody cared. Everyone was singing "Margaritaville" over and over, and "It was always 5 o'clock somewhere." The mood was high (and some people, too); laughter was everywhere. Some danced as couples, some as a group, men/women, women/women, men, whatever; everybody was dancing.

There were hamburgers and hot dogs, popcorn, and ice cream sundaes. People were still dancing at 12:00 AM, and then it was over. People broke out in spontaneous applause. Neighbors who had fought over filched fruit and parking irregularities were patting each other on the back, and smiling. How lucky we were.

People were truly grateful for the effort the party planners had expended. It represented hours of work and they realized it was worth it. The opportunity for these aging, vulnerable people to come together, dance, sing, have fun, get a little tipsy, but not overly so, was truly fantastic. Nobody got into trouble. Nobody got upset at anything. Wow!

The hit of the evening was the "limbo" contest. One resident who bent his body at a forty-five degree angle and two feet off the floor managed to worm his way under the bar. People shouted and hooted. How did he do that? Martha had not originally wanted to come. These nights were often couple affairs, and only reminded her of a life she no longer had. But she went. She had fun, and she danced until she couldn't move another step!

The finale of the evening was a "costume dress up" where each table stuffed some unsuspecting person with gee jaws of all kinds. This costumed monstrosity was to be Mrs. Jimmy Buffet. (Is there one?) The winner was embellished with huge balloons in the proper places, front top and rear bottom. A wig of crepe paper and various and sundry items affixed here and there. It was a riot. Martha laughed until she hurt. The feeling of good will, of camaraderie extended floor-to-ceiling, and wall-to-wall. Nobody wanted to go home. It was a great time and Martha was so glad she'd put her qualms aside and came. This was a big step. She had had fun without Bill, and it was OK.

# CHAPTER 16

## EARLY BIRDS

Many more laughable situations were filling Martha's memory bank. She had heard the expression "Early Birds" before but hadn't been aware of its actual significance. One couple, the Williams, had been especially kind to her. They had invited her out to dinner several times. She was comfortable with them and didn't feel like the proverbial "fifth wheel" or "third wheel" in this case.

They had usually gone out for dinner at her accustomed time, 6:30 – 7: 30 PM. This time, however, they had suggested they try out a local restaurant with an "Early Bird" special. That meant arriving and being seated before five o'clock. This seemed a bit early, but Martha thought it might be another new experience, so why not?

They picked her up at 4:30 PM, informally dressed, as everyone was in this part of Florida. Friendly and warm conversation filled the car and she felt comfortable and at home with this charming couple. They were 68 years old, from Indiana, and warm and kind to each other. The love they shared was obvious and always produced a tinge of "what if" in her heart. She pushed the thought aside and listened to the two of them banter back and forth over some fiasco at breakfast that morning.

As a couple, sadness, true tragedy, had marred their life. Sometimes their life situation had been a bit shaky, but they had survived. Martha was constantly amazed at the relationship of so many of the couples in the park. Some had grown closer; some seemed to merely tolerate each other, moving about in their individual bubbles, not ever touching.

Why, she wondered? Why the difference? Brought back into the discussion as they neared the restaurant, she pushed these thoughts aside and eagerly looked forward to a great meal and good conversation.

The place was crowded; a line snaked around the outdoor entrance. Talk was lively and seemingly happy in anticipation of two drinks for the price of one, and a good meal two dollars less than it would be after six.

This was the generation with the imprint of the "Depression" etched in their psyche. Some had lived through it and others had heard countless stories about how awful it was. This "Early Bird" menu was appealing. On the other hand, this same group of people would snap up every cheap gadget offered on TV with a "WAIT; there's more – if you call right now!" Some sheds were crammed with boxes after boxes of their cheap buys. The UPS truck stopped daily here and there around the park.

Oh, well, who's to say? The food was good, very good. The company was warm and friendly. The gaiety of the diners was apparent. The sound of laughter, of toasts, of greetings echoed throughout the room. "Early Birds" was a good-time thing. Martha thoroughly enjoyed the time and she was grateful.

# CHAPTER 17

## SNOW BIRDS

Just as Englewood is a bifurcated community, so "Snow Birds" represent a bifurcated person-hood. Florida needs them, courts and woos them, spends huge amounts of money luring and soliciting them. And so they come, mid-October to mid-April; I-75, I-95, I-10, the Sunshine Freeway filled with cars, RVs, trailers, convertibles, pulled boats, jet skis, and ATVs. Some driving erratically, some driving 40 MPH, and mostly driving the Florida natives nuts! The heaviest number come January through March, then tensions do get high!

It's a love/hate relationship. Martha compared it to the love shown by the grandfather to the first-born male in the family, and the anger felt by the other siblings. Or perhaps it was like the feeling seniors had toward blood pressure pills. They were happy with the physical result; they probably wouldn't stroke out, but they hated the fact they had to take them. That little pill represented *AGEING*. Loss of control of one's life and the approaching Big ONE, or perhaps it was like the guy with prostate problems. He wanted to keep his virility and yet the little beads they would put in there gave him a chance at life. There were more and more of these two-sided situations as time went on..

Some people in the park, the "All Year Rounders" (a precious few), believed Publix™ made the rolls smaller, the bread loaves shorter, the sliced ham and ground beef more expensive, starting November 1st. They were sure of that! The gas prices rose, ice cream cone costs went up, root beer was more costly, and fish – Holy Cow! Grouper went up to eighteen bucks a pound. Blame it on the "Snow Birds!" And so it went.

Then when November rolled around, everyone was out in their carports, ready and excited to greet the new arrivals. Pies were passed around; casseroles were given here and there. The park began to live again. The aisles in Publix™ were crowded with carts, some cars were banged into in the parking lots, the "finger" was shot by the natives, and life in Florida began anew.

Martha was looking forward to her return in October or November, and thrilled to now be a part of this process. She was rather proud to be a snow bird. At least they had wings!

# CHAPTER 18

## NEW YEAR'S EVE

Martha heard a great deal of talk about the New Year's Eve party that had been celebrated before her arrival. She was relieved she had not been a resident at that time. New Year's Eve was a special couple time. She was quite certain her daughter had been conceived on that day thirty years ago.

She heard it had been a wonderful party. One clever resident had constructed a lighted ball that was hung on the top of the flag pole. It was a three and one-half foot ball of Styrofoam, completely covered with plastic cups (six-ounce variety) and containing Christmas tree small white light bulbs. The entire thing ran off batteries and everyone was truly impressed.

A slight hitch occurred when the swivel got stuck and the ball cord was entwined with the flag cord. Persistence paid off, and an extended version of "Auld Lang Syne" was sung. Everyone had champagne—alcoholic or non-alcoholic and sixty-five of the original ninety-eight party goers had stayed awake until midnight, at least reasonably awake according to some reports.

The tables had been decorated with the usual hats, horns, and streamers. Music of the 40s, 50s, and 60s was played. People danced, some even were jitterbugging. Some were doing the Twist; some both at the same time! There was, according to all reports, a lot of participation. Of course, she heard some boggle heads popped the champagne ahead of time. One attendee was hit in the nose with a flying cork.

There was some confusion in the food line. One misguided soul was reported to have put Jell-O on his mashed potatoes thinking it was gravy. Martha heard from someone that the Jell-O mold had melted and was pretty runny, and was also a strange color. Someone else pocketed about twelve foil wrapped butter pats. That must have caused some consternation on the home front on New Year's Day!

Floyd, who was known as the "biggest kisser" in the park, made it a point to kiss every woman in attendance. Since he had imbibed a bit, he kissed one of the newer residents who sported a long pony tail. Apparently, this sign of affection was not well received! The two were separated and Herman made them shake hands. Peace was restored and the partying went on.

Martha assumed she'd be in residence for the next New Year's festivities, but at this point was unsure of what she'd do. No matter, she had survived Jimmy Buffet night so maybe she'd look at things differently when the time came around. That wasn't a decision she had to make now.

# CHAPTER 19

## PROBLEMS WITH NEIGHBORS

She discovered another weird effect of living so close together in these aluminum boxes. One day biking past the manager's office, she heard a guy yelling loudly at Paul Tyler. He was insisting his neighbor should be arrested and put in the "clink," whatever or wherever that was. He yelled that Ken, his neighbor, had stolen his lawn mower. Just this morning Ken was cutting his lawn with that lawn mower. Paul tried to calm him down.

"Now, George, you're saying that your neighbor, Ken, stole your lawn mower and is presently cutting his lawn with it?"

"Yah, that's what I'm trying to tell ya! Go arrest him!"

"George, I can't arrest him, but I'll go talk with him. OK? Just calm down, and wait 'till I get back."

Martha left, but found out later that when Paul approached Ken about it that Ken admitted it wasn't his lawn mower, but he had found it in his shed. So he decided to use it. It turned out that George had lent it to Ken a month ago, but had forgotten to whom he lent it. Well, it all got straightened out, but forgetfulness is the cause of many issues in the park. Growing old, it seems, can be pretty cruel. She remembered one of the things that the manager's wife, Betty, had told her the first time Martha visited. She said that Martha would meet many good people and feel really close to them. Then illness –the big "A,"

ALS, the big "C," cancer, or whatever would strike, and friends would die, or go to live with daughters or get stuck in a home of sorts. That would be a sad day. John Donne, the poet, said,

"That when a clod of earth falls from the shores of Europe, that Europe is the lesser for it."

And so, when someone dies or leaves here, we are the lesser for it. This came to be the reality here, and it hurt. That was a poignant side of living in a place like this. But, then every lovely thing is not forever, and yet we keep grasping for beauty. If there were no sadness, would we truly know happiness?

Annis Knakal ©

# CHAPTER 20

## RANDOM ACTS

Almost every day Martha became aware of actions taken by residents that seemed quite different and unexpected. She knew that the Boosters were run by a slate of officers and various committee members. Someone had told her that twenty percent of the residents did all the work in putting on the many activities in which she had taken part.

What surprised her, however, were the stories of individual acts, unheralded, all but unknown, but deeply caring acts. There was the Sandhill crane man. Recently a pair of Sandhill cranes was seen parading around the park shepherding a baby crane about eighteen inches tall. It was a lovely sight.

The amazing aspect of all this was Cliff's efforts to provide safe passage for the trio. They ambled twice daily from our park to the golf course across the street. They stepped very slowly, almost majestically and proudly from one side of the road to the other. Cliff would stand in the middle of the street stopping traffic, until the birds reached the other side. His friends became so concerned about him that they brought him an orange vest.

Another individual on his morning walk through the park would pick up the newspapers haphazardly tossed in the carports. He would carry them to the steps of the residents he knew had difficulty getting up and out in the morning. Of course, this action deprived Charlie of being "mooned" by his neighbor. The neighbor would reach down to pick up the local news and her teddy nightgown would hike northward! Most everyone else appreciated the walker's gesture.

Violet assumed the responsibility, unbidden, to set the book cases in order. For some reason or other, the books would be totally disarranged every few days. The hot romance novels were especially subject to disorder. Violet patiently put them in alphabetical order, as much as was possible, and tossed out the coffee stained, cover missing examples of misuse.

Then there was Herbert, the turtle man. Huge box turtles were often seen in the park. They, too, seemed to find it necessary to cross the street. Things were certainly greener on the golf course side of the street! Herbert stopped traffic to provide safe passage for the slowly moving critters. He, too, was given an orange vest. The drivers of the cars were not at all happy being stopped by a white haired octogenarian and they honked their horns and yelled. Herbert never wore his hearing aids, so he was oblivious to the racket.

The two often met at the same time and eventually they were provided with beach chairs and an umbrella. We were all proud of our orange vested crossing guards!

One event of a week ago kept running through Martha's mind. She'd felt faint at Publix™. One of her neighbors had noticed and insisted on bringing her home, and escorting her into her house. Another neighbor took a friend back to get her car. Martha fell asleep on the couch and woke up to find a casserole of ham and escalloped potatoes, green beans in mushroom sauce with friend onions on top, a Jell-O mold in the fridge and a dozen cupcakes on the counter. All from Tess. She didn't even know who Tess was! That truly amazed her. Martha was OK. She had been stripping and varnishing the molding in the living room and had inhaled too many fumes. She was so grateful to these unknown neighbors, and she had come to realize that acts like these were fairly common here.

There was Trudy who never drove to Publix™ or Wal-Mart™ without checking with her neighbors. Some of them were all but shut-ins, having given up their cars years ago. The visit provided talk time and catching up on the news of the park. Martha often wondered how those almost entirely confined to their unit knew everything that was going on in the park. There was some sort of "underground" relay system that spread the news.

Madie was the laundry pick-up person. The managers kept the laundry clean and the appliances in good running order. Madie took care of little things. She had placed a clothes line near the side wall. Here she hung socks left in the laundry tubs or the dryers. Martha noticed three men's black socks of different ankle length, one white golf sock, and one argyle sock. But what was truly amazing however, was the pair of panty hose size 3X, hung on a different line. That item created all sorts of wonderment. George, the connoisseur of derrieres, commented that no one in the park was large enough for it. Hugh added that if they found out who it belonged to, that's where he would go in a wind storm.

The mystery was solved. Winston from Kingston, Ontario, not Churchill, had purchased the item to place over his lime tree. He heard that when the tree blossomed, a severe drop in temperature would kill the blossoms. He was certain the thermometer would be at freezing temperatures any day. He had confused Celsius and Fahrenheit. Everyone laughed, because lime trees have serious thorns. The panty hose were pretty badly damaged, and Winston had no idea how they ended up in the laundry. Martha guessed his wife was responsible.

Another person kept the stove in the Rec Hall kitchen spotless. Someone else worked on cleaning the fridge. Angie planted and cared for flowers in the planters near the Rec Hall and the laundry. Bill cared for the Friendship garden near the entrance of the park. All these little jobs were filled by people who expected no reward, no acknowledgment, no applause. They did it not just to fill their empty days with useful activities, but rather to make their living space feel like their home.

Because of the efforts of these people and the many unrecognized people, the space was home! Thank you Live Oaks!

# CHAPTER 21

## MAN/WOMAN STUFF

One side plot Martha became aware of in mobile park living was the male/female interplay. Early on she had sensed the predatory nature of a population out of balance –too many females per male. She had recognized it as the high school phenomenon of the need to be needed by someone. There was an additional side bar, however.

A new resident, a younger woman, was considered disparagingly, a "trophy wife." Imagine a trophy wife in a modest mobile home park. She had come to live winters here with her older husband. As time went on, the couple separated and the younger woman stayed in the park. She was very attractive, blonde, slim, and seemed to possess the necessary accouterments. The early AM old men's walking club spent many morning hours checking out her unit – the citrus trees, the hibiscus, the backyard – all with genuine interest.

Later on, we heard that she had developed a sometime nightly relationship with a very attractive younger man. Thus, there was a renewed interest in her lifestyle and her late night companion. It was almost comical chancing upon the group of five or six paunchy, bald, old men, furtively looking, intensely listening, and certainly reviewing in their minds a past that no longer existed.

One of the saddest parts of growing old is realizing that the vibrant memories of what was, no longer exits in any degree of vibrancy. Memories are wonderful; memories don't make up for what is lost. Perhaps that is the very essence of mobile park living. By banding together, these people hope to refill the empty places. To rekindle where there is no longer a flame to light, to share the declining years with each other. It may be that pot lucks and Booster meetings and shuffle board and rummage sales are not shadowy efforts at life. It could be that this life takes on a form of its own, that the community of sharing does rekindle the flame, and that the flame did exist. Shared love and concern could fill the void or emptiness; at least it was a valid reason to try. And Martha realized that this was the path she had been seeking.

On the opposite side of the loving kindness of these neighbors was another puzzling fact of life. One of the obvious situations Martha encountered as she adjusted to life in the park was a universal life experience for a widow in a couple-society. Of course, in most parks there were more widows than widowers. It was still a barrier, however.

The change from couple hood to widowhood is a soul wrenching dislocation. Women you barely know regard you with suspicion. Those with husbands consider you a threat even though you aren't. Women who have lived here longer consider they have first dibs for any single man who shows up, and feel you should get at the back of the line.

It was pretty silly because Martha was still facing the trauma of Bill's illness and death, and certainly not in the sex race. It seemed endemic, however, and Martha soon realized where she was welcome and where she was considered a threat. It was sort of like high school all over again. That was just another lesson to be learned in her new lifestyle situation. She'd have to talk to Beth about that when she arrived. Frankly, there wasn't a single male resident in the park who caused a ripple. Now, the young guy cutting the grass – that was something else! She was kidding of course, but it was funny. Life presented so many facets and twists and turns. What had seemed to be the most normal place to be normal in the world wasn't necessarily normal. Life was really an ever changing and challenging reality.

# CHAPTER 22

# OTHER ISSUES

---

Of course beyond the romances, the weddings, the run-a-ways, there were still more sexual issues, here and everywhere. The predominant age of residents produced a generation with an attitude that was "strabismic' concerning sexual matters. Certainly, that, too, was in a transitional process, more tolerant, more aware of changing mores. Was everyone on the same page? Of course not. Martha's history back in Ohio represented the changing times. Her closest friend at work was a lesbian. Martha had been totally unaware for years, and when she heard about it, her first thought was, that she valued her all the more because of how she courageously lived her life. For the person she, had known as friend changing the label didn't change what was inside.

In the park she discovered the most caring, giving couple was gay. One of the pair was the most intelligent and aware person she had ever known. Again the garden grew and she felt grateful for the beauty it represented in her life. Some residents were cold and practiced the art of avoidance. Most accepted what was, and were grateful for the gifts of concern this twosome so freely gave. Quite frankly, they were a lot easier to be with than the Gambles who constantly berated another, loudly and in public.

Then of course, there was Matt and his dog, a huge Dalmatian. They walked the park, greeting all with a smile and picking up the "doggy doo." Matt was a wood carver and produced creations of unbelievable beauty. So it seems there were all sorts of couplings, even some late at night meetings on the docks, hidden from view. Who cared? We were all adults Martha thought, and if some behaved like teenagers or worse, what matter that?

Maybe tolerance came with the gray hair and the wrinkles, and the brown spots. Something should! She found the park a micro cosmic thing that contained all the issues facing modern society – the diesel truck versus the Ford Focus, the Bush hater versus the Bush supporter, the vegans versus the sirloin on the grill group, the Bible thumpers versus the nonbelievers. She truly believed each person had the right to be his or her individual self. Why not? Wasn't there strength in our diversity? It certainly made life interesting.

## CHAPTER 23

## THE OTHER SIDE OF THE EARLY MORNING WALKING GROUP

During the past few months, Martha had become somewhat adjusted to the oft ribald, inappropriate remarks and suggestive insinuations of the early morning walking group. They banded together and always seemed able to say something that set her off. Why did they need to pretend to be so macho? She was not at all at ease in their presence and they were aware of it. That apparently caused them to tease her all the more. So she avoided them as much as she could and pushed aside the inane remarks they constantly inserted in any discussion of any topic—always with a sexual content.

Then one day at golf, she witnessed another side of the group, a side she would not have believed existed. She was approaching the 12th hole in her golf cart, riding with her new friend, Mae. She noticed a group of guys on the left. Someone was lying in the grass near a sand trap.

"Let's check that out," said Mae, and off they went.

"What's going on? Shouted Martha.

"It's OK, Martha; we've got it under control. Would you use your cell phone to call the club house? Fred fainted and we need to get him to the hospital," said Jim.

"He's breathing, isn't he? I know CPR."

"Yes, he's breathing. Please call! Hurry!"

So Martha called the club house and in about ten minutes, an ambulance came tearing down the fairway.

Martha could not help but notice how gentle they were with Fred. And he wasn't one of the "walking group." Their voices were kind and supportive. He seemed to come to a little, and Jim said,

"Not to worry. Relax now. I'll drive the car back. I'll get Virginia" (Fred's wife) "and take her to the emergency room."
They were all involved in taking care of Fred. They were amazingly kind.

Later, Martha recalled the incident and now had a different view of the group. They had been successful businessmen, fire fighters, GM workers. They had been hunters and fishermen, and most of them ex-jocks. They had been husbands and fathers and played the role life assigned them. Now, they were no longer working, no longer bringing in a salary, no longer giving orders, seemingly no longer important fixtures in the world of business, in their former neighborhood, in the family patriarch role, no longer needed as before.

The feminist movement never had hit the mobile home park with full force, Martha realized. It had nudged it a bit, however. So when one of the group had ordered the "little woman" or the "missus" to do this or fetch that, now she was apt to mutter. "I'm busy; do it yourself," or pretend she didn't hear him. Since his hearing wasn't all that great anyway, she got away with it. Thus, even at home they were no longer masters of the universe. She wasn't terribly sad about that reality. But she did have a better understanding of their attitudes. They, too, like everyone else, faced the encroaching impotence, the lack of control over their own destiny.

She still didn't like their off color asides. They still annoyed the heck out of her, but she had a little kinder view now.

# CHAPTER 24

## FISHING

---

Martha soon discovered that the subject of fishing would provoke instantaneous reaction. Sometimes this seemed to be an all but rabid response. Because of the location of the park near the south end of a peninsula in Southwest Florida, the Gulf of Mexico was close at hand. The Inter-Coastal Waterway (ICW) was even closer. Thus, a boat of whatever size could leave a resident's dock and be in the ICW in a matter of minutes. And leave they did! Fourteen-foot aluminum boats with 9.9 horse power motors to 22 foot vessels with twin 250 horse power engines, kayaks, canoeists, ski doers all headed out. At times it was quite a flotilla!

Fishing was the reason many residents chose this location. Fishing truly was the life force of many who lived here. This sport, however, involved much more than the word implied. There were noisy discussions and sometimes near violent arguments over the choice of bait—live vs. artificial, followed by the type of reel—open, closed, spin casting or perhaps it was the length and type of leaders, the color and size of bobbers. Usually this brought sneers from the pure fisher people—bobbers—that's for wimps. Of course, sinkers were discussed with preferences for one type or the other. Then the length of rods—regular versus ultra lite—that discussion turned even the most peaceful person into a raving maniac.

Where to fish?  Where not to fish?  Close to shore preferred by many, nine to thirty miles out the chosen site for the hardy few.  The latter group went that far to catch the one per day limit of grouper.  Their wives shook their heads in wonderment.  Publix™ grouper were far cheaper.

Of course the length and size limit presented a real problem.  Most species proscribed length was to the fork of the tail.  Martha heard that Phil, a three hundred pound New Englander, was known to stomp on the fish until the desired length was reached.  Often a grouper became a pompano—a strange looking fish!

The prize fish in the park was the majestic snook.  This species was a fighter, difficult to catch, and more difficult to bring in.  One did not have to go out miles and miles as they could be found nearby.  Even the canals produced a few when the water was cold further out.  They were delicious and loved by all.  A meal of fried snook, home fries, cole slaw and key lime pie was a feast fit for a king.

The number one fisherman in the park was Leo.  He fished every day.  His clothes reeked of fish.  His living area smelled of fish and fish scales trailed him wherever he walked.  He wouldn't clean them and he wouldn't eat them, but he caught them.  He readily and willingly gave his entire catch to all he met.  Fishy smelling or not he was a most popular man in the park.  Any one would welcome and gladly clean these beauties and of course, get their wife to prepare them.

Fish stories all but took over the Booster meetings on many an occasion.  Many refused to divulge their favorite fishing hole.  Some deliberately provided false information.  One special chapter of Park lore concerned Phil.

Phil had hooked into a Tarpon by mistake.  A special stamp was required to fish for this species and it was also advisable to have deep sea fishing equipment.  Phil was using a Zepco™ reel with a 10# test line. The story was that Phil had hooked an eighty-five pound or so Tarpon.  It dragged Phil around Little Gasparilla Island two times.  He should have let go of the rod, but Phil was known to be stubborn.  On the final turn he reluctantly let go and was beached.

Fortunately his cell phone survived and an armada of park residents showed up to rescue a bruised and battered Phil.  He was bloody, but unbroken.  No one knew what happened to the Tarpon or the rod and reel.

So it seemed that the fascination with fishing and all its related facets was nearly religious in nature. Most of the women shook their heads in wonder as they headed out to the mall and a trip to Macy's™.  Either activity filled their days and added a sense of vibrancy to their lives—well, it beat bingo!

# CHAPTER 25

## TO CHURCH OR NOT TO CHURCH

Martha had always considered it strange that good friends could become so argumentative and even angry at the subjects of religion and politics. So she avoided discussions in either area. Her life experience had proved that her conclusions were valid. She had witnessed friendly neighborhoods turned into seas of discontent over these issues. People were not talking to each other, fences were installed, and a pall fell over the area. What a terrible shame she thought.

Live Oaks Park had had a church in a separate room of the Rec Hall from its inception. Church service was held every Sunday from November first until Easter Sunday. The service was rather non-denominational, but certainly Bible oriented. Well, weren't most churches that way?

Church attendances seemed to fall off a bit because the minister was aging and quite ill. Some of the staunchest supporters had died, or moved out. The demographic makeup of the park was in transition. So the church issue was a touchy subject.

One of the few problems that evolved from having church on Sunday at 9:00 AM was getting the Rec Hall cleaned and the church room reset with the chairs exactly in a row, the pulpit tilted at precisely the right angle, and the piano located correctly. The organ no longer functioned. The Sunday morning after the Rummage Sale or the Sunday morning after Jimmy Buffet night presented a few problems for the bleary eyed attendees.

Whatever, the situation was in limbo. Martha had decided early on she wouldn't offer any opinion one way or other. She was comfortable at the local church she had discovered. Martha felt that from its inception we Americans have found ourselves in an awful quagmire dealing with the place of the church and religion in our community life. Decisions in this area were beyond her ken and/or her interest. Sometimes, silence was indeed golden.

Annis Knokal ©

## CHAPTER 26

## ROMANCE, SEX AND OTHER THINGS

Nothing sets the park a twitter more than the whisper of romance, illicit or otherwise. The big subject of the coffee hour was the "Wedding." One long -term resident and a short- term person had decided to tie the knot. The wedding was to take place in the Recreation Hall two weeks hence. Golf carts and three-wheeler bikes were flying all over the park. Everyone was agog and a gaga.

The color scheme was announced with mixed reviews: violet and soft green. Everyone had an opinion. Who was to be the matron of honor, the best man, the minister? So many questions, not many answers. The subject of a honeymoon destination had the early AM old duffers walking group so jazzed they could hardly manage half a lap.

What time would it be? What would they serve? Would there be champagne? People in the park had just recovered from the recent separation of one long- term couple. The husband all of seventy-two years had run off with the Avon Lady who lived at A84. Everyone had thought she was pretty suspicious right along.

Well, now all that talk had died down a bit. Now a wedding was on the docket. The shady lovers' elopement faded into park history, and the wedding took first place in the hearts and minds of all. It didn't matter how old one was, the prospect of love touching two hearts was the age-old manna from heaven. There was a huge sigh of wonderment, a renewed gasp of hope, a smile that lit every-one's eyes, an energizing of spirit.

We were enthralled. We were in love and we were as giddy as adolescents. Why? Why not? Were we too old to contemplate a couple joining their lives, giving love and comfort to each other? Of course not! In a special way, we were all connected. We were all participants in this process.

The wedding was beautiful. True, the soloist was a bit off key, but the groom had forgotten his hearing aid, and the bride was too enchanted to notice. The luncheon that followed was enjoyed by all – egg salad and ham sand-wiches, pickles and olives, and the cake! Three tiers with a plastic old white haired couple on top! The best man had too much champagne and fell over before he finished his comments, but he wasn't hurt. And then they left and everyone went home—happy for them, happy to be a part of life's force. What a beautiful feeling! We were all in love with love.

# CHAPTER 27

# GREEN SIDE UP

Another story that amused Martha was the history of getting a pool installed in the park. A few members had talked and pushed and nudged and argued and finally reached the magic number of forty-eight potential members. The pool cost $48,000, and the organizers needed a thousand dollars from forty-eight people to reach that goal, or the pool wouldn't be built. It was a tough sell.

That may not sound like a difficult proposal but it was. Martha had come to realize that senior citizens are as adverse to change as high school kids.

"Why do we need a pool? You can swim in the gulf."

"They put chlorine in pools. That's bad for you. It ruins your suits, your hair."

"You knew there wasn't a pool when you moved in? Why did you come here?"

"It will be noisy. They'll drip all over the Rec Hall."

"It will overflow into the pool room," and on and on. There were definitely people opposed.

Little by little, however, the monies were accumulated. A pool installer hired. There was much discussion over tile, cage, and rules. The Rule Committee had come up with twenty-three rules. One of the difficult rules concerned the issue of diapers.

Grandkids were often visitors and pool members were worried about the babies in diapers. Martha thought that a bit peculiar since kids without diapers often peed in pools. The big issue concerned adults with those things. Incontinence certainly was not an unknown condition. Martha was glad she hadn't been a resident then. Diapers were outlawed, but no age limit was posted. She was glad she had not been on the Rules Committee.

The construction began—more complaints. Trucks, dirt, dust; the bird pole had to be moved. But little by little, the pool took shape. People continued to gripe but not as loudly.

After the sod had been laid, covering up the damage done to the original area, large spots of open dirt remained. That was bad. A committee was formed to use the large pile of sod that remained to cover those areas. About six people showed up. One of them, whose name was forgotten, was in the initial stages of Alzheimer's. He was a willing worker, but at times could become very confused. They began the chant as they formed a chain gang of sod bearers, "Green side up, brown side down."

Soon everyone was singing the verse. The forgetful one was singing just as lustily as any of them. A member of the group followed behind this gentleman, flipping the sod to the green side up!

As Martha listened to the story, she was again touched by the mixture of humor and pathos that was so much of the life story of the park, and the kindness.

# CHAPTER 28

## SHUFFLE -BOARD, GOLF

Is there a mobile home park in Florida that doesn't have a shuffle -board court? Probably not. Martha wasn't terribly eager about getting involved in that activity. She had been encouraged by her neighbor, Mabel, and decided she better give it a try. What occurred, Martha had come to realize, wasn't the games or the activities that counted here. Everyone who participated in these events was aware actually, intuitively, or subconsciously of the physical limitations of the players. Nothing was said; nothing was overt. It just was. Rules were changed; adjustments were made; people were assisted subtly. Nothing was made of it, but it happened. Martha was intrigued by the whole process. She had observed it many times, even in setting up the tables for an event. Now on the shuffle -board court it became truly noticeable, at least to her.

In shuffle- board, the team of two might be comprised of one member in an electric wheelchair. Or, perhaps, the other team might have a member missing an arm. At first it bothered Martha to see some of her neighbors so physically damaged. She soon changed her mind. The guy in the wheel chair knocked her disc out of the scoring spot on his first shot! The armless guy could shoot an inward or outward curve at will with his good arm!

Marie who had macular degeneration so bad she could not see anyone's face was one of the best shots in the group. The able bodied folks were in awe of these three.

And so it went with all the so-called physically challenged citizens in the park. Certainly their handicaps were readily apparent, but their participation was just as keen as anyone's. Their will to win and to do well was as strong as when they were whole, and not challenged.

Willi told her he could hear the clicks of the discs although he couldn't hear voices. He could determine what kind of shot it was by the sound. All in all, Martha was overwhelmed by what these people could do. They played a far better game than she ever hoped to do.

Willi had called out to her one day.

"Hey, Martha, you're doing OK!"

"You can tell?"

"Sure, I think your holding the cue too tightly; loosen up a little. You'll get there."

Marie piped up.

"She's from Ohio; she's got that Buckeye spirit, don't you, Martha?"

"I guess I do. I try to."

"Well, keep it up," responded Marie.

Words of encouragement from these so called "challenged" people. How powerful was that?

The same applied to golf. One member of her group last week had a wooden leg. He hit the longest drive. One woman wore a back brace and she got close to the pin on three of the short holes. Of course, there were a few drawbacks. She recalled the incident with Fred who had passed out.

Then, the week before that she had played with Anthony from Minnesota. He was probably the oldest player in the group. Because he was eighty-one, he could hit off the ladies tee. On the seventh hole, a short one hundred and ten yards, Martha got up and hit her seven wood. She missed the green, but was close. Returning her club to her golf bag and sitting down in the cart, she noticed Anthony was still sitting there, staring straight ahead.

"Hey, Anthony, it's your turn. You're up." No response.

"Come on, Anthony, we're lagging behind." Still no response. She poked him in the shoulder, still nothing.

"Hey, guys," she shouted to the other two members of her foursome. "Please come here. We may have a problem." Martha was really worried.

"Oh, that's just Anthony," one the guys replied. "He just checks out once in a while."

"Anthony," he shouted and came over and shook him. "Come on; get up there."

"Who … Who … Oh, sorry guys; I was just thinking about my investments."

"Yeah, sure, we know."

And so it went, all kinds of people, all kinds of situations, and everyone seemed to take it all in stride. What a place!

# CHAPTER 29

## CHARLIE, FRANCES, JEAN, AND IVAN

No, these aren't the names of park residents. These are the names of hurricanes that hit southwest Florida in 2004. Martha wasn't living there then, but she heard countless stories from those who had lived through it. Often time, those telling of their experience would have shaking hands and coffee would spill. No matter, the stories were gripping, amazingly gripping.

She heard of carports blown apart, of parts of roofs blown into the walls of units a block away. She heard of a smashed house and the ones on either side, untouched. There was talk of globs of pink insulation hanging from the leafless, fruitless branches of citrus trees. Another spoke of the flotsam and jetsam floating in the canals—patio furniture, grills, wind chimes, three wheeler bikes, and on and on.

Through all the retelling, there was beneath all the words, a sense of wonderment. How did some houses remain untouched? Why did some roofs fly off and others, exactly the same, remain fixed. The worst effect beyond the wind damage was the rain, torrential rain. There were not enough blue tarps in all of Florida to protect those roofless units. And then, of course, came mold, lung-destroying mold.

Even beyond wonderment and the unanswered questions, however, had been the sense of powerlessness—impotency to fight the power of the wind over the water.

People from the north said it was like driving a car on icy roads, and losing control with a telephone pole in your path, or holding the hand of the love of your life when you had absolutely no control of the events facing you. That's a pretty sobering realization; that's life in it rawest form.

Then after these deep thoughts of reflection, the conversation would turn to another type of wonderment. Their amazement at the joint effort everyone in the park put forth. One resident drove down from Ohio with a truck load of plywood and cartons of duct tape. The later was more valuable than gold!

One lady combined all the surviving grills and cooked everything that had been left in their freezers by the departing snow birds. Night after night, they ate supper that way. The power was out; it was ninety-five degrees and ninety percent humidity. No air conditioning or fans, no water, no phones. The only respite was the swimming pool for the workers who were collecting debris, and car ports, and roofs, and walls. Everyone pitched in. Some of the ladies who couldn't do the heavy lifting work walked up and down the roads collecting nails, screws, pieces of metal, and glass, as tires were punctured everywhere everyday.

This turned out not to matter too much at first because there was no gas, and nowhere to go. Someone whose car kept functioning somehow carted in countless bags of ice, milk, Gatorade™, and beer. People who had never communicated before were seen slapping each other on the back after a really tough job had been completed. There were a lot hugs and a vibrant sense of good will.

Someone suggested a sing-a-long after the communal supper, but everyone was too pooped to participate.

They also realized that without air conditioning or fans there would be many long tough nights. In addition, they were discovering muscle aches and pains where they hadn't felt them in years. Through it all, however, they felt good. Good about themselves, good about each other, and good about their park. They had every intention of bragging about the efforts expended by all when they talked to their kids—whenever the phones started working again!

Forty years had passed without a storm of that proportion. This one was forever etched in the hearts and minds of those who had lived through it. They were proud of their efforts. They had a right to be!

# CHAPTER 30

# POKER, PINOCLE, PETTINESS, AND PETULANCE

Cards were big at Live Oaks. There was women's poker, men's poker, bridge, canasta, euchre, and hand and foot. There was also talk about Mexican Dominos joining the card game list. This generation, pre-TV, had grown up playing cards. It was an inexpensive family activity and enjoyed by the early married couples. Later it was a staple of family life on low budgets and now by senior citizens all over Florida. Thus, these activities continued into old age. As in any community, however, emotions often ran high. The men's poker table was where most of the fire works erupted. Sometimes these eruptions were pretty loud and nasty. Martha found it difficult to understand how these low stakes games would bring out such raw emotions.

Last Wednesday night she heard had been especially ugly. Joe got very upset because of Matt's constant raises. He also accused Matt of looking at his cards when he made one of his frequent trips to the bathroom. Frequent bathroom trips were not unusual in this age group. Anyway, Joe pushed back his chair, stood up, and shouted,

"You're a prick."

It was also apparent that Joe had a "a few too many cocktails" before he arrived. Matt was really a soft spoken guy who was so startled by Joe's outburst that he started to shake.

Then Fred, who was often a peace maker, spoke up and said,

"Joe, sit down and zip your lip."

Joe was so angry and out of control that he thought Fred said his zipper was down, and Joe yelled,

"My zipper is my own business."

Then Howie stood up and said,

"Joe, you're acting like a jerk! Calm down and shut up."

Well, that didn't go over very well and Joe's flailing arms knocked over Fred's can of Coke. Things then went from bad to worse. Two of the ladies who were playing poker in the pool room ran in and yelled at them,

"Be quiet!" telling them, "You're ruining our game!"

Sue Longwood, the former high school principal, put her arm on Joe's back and quite neatly shoved him down in his chair. Silence followed.

"Now, guys, that's enough. If you can't behave like adults, then go to the American Legion Post. They'll kick you out, too. Grow up!"

A few sheepish looks went around the table. Joe didn't say another word, and the group broke up and drifted back home, chagrined, chastened, and silent. By comparison, euchre, bridge, canasta, and the other games were pretty mild and very popular.

# CHAPTER 31

## MAE

What is more wonderful than finding a good friend! Martha pondered that thought as she got herself ready to meet Mae. Their plans included hitting the food court, checking out *Books a Million*, and then taking in a movie. She had met Mae at one of the various committee meetings she had attended. Martha noticed her immediately as she had that puzzled look on her face when someone pontificated on the way something was to be done for the coming event. It wasn't exactly a smirk, but it was close to it. Actually, it was probably a "My gosh, they can't be serious!"

They were given the job of purchasing the items for the upcoming party, a Valentine's Day dinner and dance. Martha had volunteered to help set up but she decided she wouldn't stay—too painful. She soon discovered Mae had the same plan in mind. She later spent some time with her and found her to be a vital, humorous, and wonderful human being.

Mae had also been a teacher, Social Studies middle school. Martha had always considered that age group the most difficult and demanding level to teach, but Mae had loved it. She and her husband, Myron, had celebrated thirty-six years of married life, raised five kids, and had planned on taking early retirement at age sixty-two years. Her husband was a school administrator in the same district. Things were all under control, Mae thought.

Involved in retirement procedures, parties, the end of the school year, and her oldest kid's divorce, she was completely unaware of Myron's state of mind. It was a terrible shock to her to hear him announce as they arrived home from yet another retirement party, that he wanted a divorce.

My God, a divorce! How could that be? What was worse, he was involved with and had decided to marry her niece who had been a flower girl at their wedding thirty six years ago! Mae told Martha she almost lost it. She fell into a deep depression. Her kids took sides. The one getting a divorce, their oldest daughter, sided with her dad.

All the retirement plans went out the window. Mae was hurt, angry, all but beside herself. The anger actually helped. It gave her the resolve to keep on, to get through it. Martha couldn't help but realize that they both lost their husbands, but in totally different ways. Her Bill faded away from her, but his leaving was not by choice. Myron chose his departure. In reality, Martha and Mae were both left alone.

They found the comparison of their lives strangely endearing. Different, but the same. There was a bond of understanding that formed between them. Martha was so very grateful for that. More importantly however, she was grateful for the laughter they shared. They had survived!

Annis Knakal ©

# CHAPTER 32

## PANCAKE BREAKFASTS

Martha soon discovered that along with Pot-Lucks, Early Bird Dining, and Booster Meetings, the Pancake Breakfast ranked right up there in importance. The purpose, of course, was to raise money for the Booster Club. That fund would be used to pay for the cleaning of the hall, and bathroom. The monies raised from all the dinners, and other events would also buy equipment for the kitchen and Rec Hall, take care of the shuffle-board court, and tune the piano.

The "real" purpose was the gathering of the residents between 7:30 and 10:00 AM to eat pancakes and sausages, scrambled eggs, juice, and coffee and to socialize—to be together. To truly enjoy each other's company, all for $3.50. It was a good time for all.

Martha had volunteered for the February breakfast. She was given the job of table setup; a function she realized was assigned to new comers. She could handle that—two creamers, two sugars, pitchers, cups, napkins. Maybe next season she'd be moved up to coffee server!

She opened the door of the Rec Hall at 6:50 AM and was met by a cloud of black smoke. She couldn't see a thing and the smoke made her eyes water. The stuff was pouring out of the kitchen. It seems the old grill hadn't been thoroughly cleaned and since George had forgotten his bifocals, he had fired the thing up without checking!

People were yelling and choking, and George was cussing. Ed ran past her shouting,

"I'm going to get some fans!"

And off he went, his golf cart at max speed. Slowly the overhead fans began to clear the air and the preparations continued.

That wasn't the only incident of the day, however. They discovered they were short a few dozen eggs, as the egg cartons in the fridge were empty. That caused quite a discussion. Why empty cartons? So, two of the volunteers left to run around the park collecting eggs. On their return, one of them bumped into the cart carrying fans, and eggs went flying all over the parking lot! Martha looked out the window and couldn't stop laughing. George was furious!

An argument started in the kitchen about putting bacon pieces or diced ham in the scrambled eggs. Since there wasn't any ham in the fridge that was quickly settled. It flared up again over the issue of green and red, diced pepper as an addition. Josie, who found all these discussions silly beyond belief, playfully placed a dab of pancake dough on Herman's nose, as he was the loudest. Herman didn't find that funny at all, and shot a whole tablespoon of Krusteaz™ mix at Josie. Soon, pandemonium developed, and everyone began throwing dough at everyone else!

Those working in the Hall ran into the kitchen to see what was going on and soon joined in the bedlam, Martha included. Most everyone was streaked with the white stuff. The pancake flipper was gamely forging ahead, ignoring the craziness all around him. Pretty quickly, the floor became quite slippery, and amidst all the confusion,

Herman slid head first into the scrambled egg preparer. The bowl she was beating eggs in tipped over and the stuff ran all over the floor. Gertie was heard to whisper,

"Oh, my goodness." Herman's words could not be printed and he stalked out in a huff.

There was a brief moment of silence and then laughter burst out, crazy, hilarious laughter. Order was finally restored. Pancakes, a limited amount of scrambled eggs, sausages, orange juice, and coffee were served. The profit margin was a lot less that February day. The brief but crazy free-for-all had lightened everyone's spirits. The kitchen was a mess. Everyone needed a shower and clean clothes.

Martha realized that even senior citizens needed to let loose once in a while and act like kids. The crew ate afterward, then cleaned up while the laughter continued. Martha went home, showered and thought about the morning. When had she had so much mindless fun? That group had jelled; they had come through the "war" together. They were veterans. They were special. Oh, would she love a DVD of that!

# CHAPTER 33

## IT'S OFF TO WORK WE GO

One issue that Martha had never even contemplated was the back-to-work syndrome. Some couples retired before their Medicare kicked in. They were justifiably scared to death of the possible, if not certainty, of medical expenses. Many were working at jobs they never would have considered during their working years. These jobs were definitely below their skill and experience level, but they had medical benefits.

One person Martha knew drove people to and from the airports. They used their own cars, bought their own gas, but were employed by a company providing this service. Another resident she had met drove a school bus. Martha decided she'd rather join the Mexican illegals picking strawberries, than do that! After all, she had worked in a high school. She remembered the potential for mayhem that age provided. Another neighbor worked on the bridge to the island. He told her he had his ups and downs. Martha didn't know how to respond to that.

Other park people volunteered. One guy went to the Humane Society two times a week and walked the dogs. He couldn't have a dog in his row—a rule that seemed quite cruel to Martha. He told her he went to the dogs twice a week. What was it with these guys?

Others volunteered at the hospital, still more in the library. They were pleased to be helping out and especially enjoyed the thank you dinners that followed every six months. One woman counted birds. That struck Martha as a rare job, but a fellow behind her unit was responsible for watching out for turtles and their nesting places. It seemed there was a niche for everyone. There was a lot that needed to be done.

Martha thought that next year she'd offer to help out at the high school. She had enough credits and experience to be a tutor for kids in trouble with English, especially the non-English speaking. Sometimes following a Booster Meeting, she thought maybe some people in the park could use a little tutoring, too!

It was apparent to her that no one needed to be bored. There were nursing rehabilitative places, extended-care facilities all over the place—it was Florida! She found the willingness of neighbors to help out so many, a very nurturing thing. They were good people.

She especially thought of Vince. He had been the only World War II prisoner of war veteran in the park. He had been severely traumatized and injured in the Far East part of the war. Strangely enough, however, he was the kindest, softest spoken of men. He rode his three-wheeler around the park, talking to all with a smile on his face. He would help anyone in need. He died near the end of the season. The flag ceremony brought tears to Martha's eyes.

Ernie was there, of course, saluting. He saw Martha, pedaled over and said,

"Don't cry, missus. Vince was a good man. He was in pain every hour of every day, and he deserved to be at peace. He earned it."

Martha nodded her head, but the tears flowed anyway.

"It's OK, Ernie. I'm proud I got to know him. He was, indeed, a good man."

So from the dog man, the bridge man, the turtle and bird watchers, the hospital/library volunteers, and Vince, they served. Her little area of Florida was the better for it. These people had lived difficult lives, had been hard working throughout their lives. Yet now, they still had the time and the heart to give to others. Pretty remarkable, when you think about it.

# CHAPTER 34

# THE PILL COUNTERS

Martha found that any coffee hour she attended included conversation about the number of prescriptions everyone took daily. Some brought in their pill bottles and lined them up in a row next to their caffeine-free coffee. They counted each out loud. The one with the most bottles was the winner. Later it became apparent that Steve had included his aspirin bottle in the total count. That was a no-no. So Steve had to surrender his free doughnut to Melinda. She refused it, however, because Steve had taken a bite out of it. Then someone suggested that Melinda's count included a night time sleeping pill, Tylenol PM ™, and the argument went on. Now, no over-the-counter pills were to be counted. Phil became the winner but the doughnuts were gone. So it was an empty win!

And the counting went on. And it seemed sad, the fixation on prescriptions. So far, only one man had included his Viagra ™ bottle. Wow, that produced quite a reaction. After the meeting, the early morning walking group was seen surrounding the Viagra guy, engaged in serious conversation.

Life was never dull in a mobile home park. Martha was continually amazed at the intense preoccupation with prescriptions and operations, all described in detail along with colonoscopies, endoscopies, doctor visits, and the prevailing opinion on who provided the best medical service. This sharing of opinion could erupt into volcanic arguments; people defended their medical practitioners with vehemence. It got pretty hectic that morning.

Martha was rather ignored as she hadn't brought any pill bottles. She preferred to keep the few she took private. She wasn't a member of the pill club. It was rather sad but it was a fact of life. These people were living proof of the life giving power of pharmaceutical progress.

# CHAPTER 35

# THE CURB

While there were so many things to laugh about, to smile at, there were times so sad they seemed unbearably crushing. When someone died or had to leave for whatever reason, the unit had to be emptied. Ready for the next resident.

The kids came down. Many of the items at the curb were older than them. They didn't want the old stereo, the old prints, the cameras, nothing was digital or fiber optic here. The furniture was Ethan Allen copies from the 70s. The dining room set was Faux French Provincial. The family up north had no use for any of their parents' stuff. It was old, used, no value, too costly to move anything back home. So it all ended up piled up on the curb in front of the unit. There were bowling trophies, old gold clubs, knitting, macramé supplies, crocheted throws, empty gallon jugs, foot stools, oil paint cans, and on and on. The pile of stuff was six foot high and six foot wide. It represented the years they had together and the kids didn't want any of it. What a sad situation Martha thought. Then little by little three-wheeler bikes appeared; golf carts drove by; cars slowly stopped.

The pile of seemingly unwanted stuff began to diminish, and in a short while most everything was gone. Martha found this incredulously moving and sad. Then thinking about it further, she realized it was the continuum of mobile park life. We absorbed each other's stuff as we had absorbed and shared each other's presence. The stuff moved out and assumed life in another person's home. It was all at once eerie and comforting. She was no longer so sad.

As she got ready to leave, she saw Ernie approaching pulling a cart behind his three wheeler.

"Hi, Martha!"

"Hi, Ernie!"

"Did you take anything Martha?" It's good luck ya' know."

No, I didn't know that. What have you got in your cart? Looks like books."

"It's a 1977 *World Book* set. I'm really excited about that! Ya' know most of the stuff is repeated year after year, so there's a lot of stuff to read about.

"Good thinking, Ernie."

An off Martha went, another chapter in her new life waiting to happen!

# CHAPTER 36

## THE RUMMAGE SALE

Next to a wedding in the park, nothing elicits more excitement and controversy than the annual Rummage Sale! It's usually held toward the end of March. At this time, the Snow Birds are beginning to think about the trip north. This thinking involves decision making: What to take back? What will fit in the car? What to do if we decide to fly? Oh, what a time that can be!

Many residents shop at flea markets and garage sales every Saturday. They also pick up countless items left on the curb on trash day, and when units are emptied out. There are no basements, and space above the ceiling is not available; plus it is usually so moldy no one would consider it.

Well, of course, there has to be a committee. Originally the function of the Ladies Club, it has lately come under the auspices of the joint control, Boosters and Ladies Club, not too happily at times!

There are people designated to pick up the stuff, others to sort and price—an arduous job, set up tables, arrange for a bake sale, others to notify the papers, and put the signs, and friendly Ernie to direct traffic and parking. It is time consuming, exhaustive BIG DEAL and not without controversy.

Problem number one: Would the workers have first dibs on the stuff? Big argument on both sides of the issue—really strong feelings. The entire issue was a bit silly as ninety percent of the stuff was the same stuff sold last year, the year before that, and the year before that! Certainly there were never items of great value—old toasters, coffee pots from the 60s, old mix masters, rusty heating units, a zoot suit or two, polyester pants and jackets, and on and on.

One of the major jobs was picking through the clothes. Unfortunately dirty necks were not limited to coal miners. Incontinence was a major problem. It was decided to use the "nose" test. One bag of clothing caused a great deal of discussion. All the clothes in that bag smelled of vanilla.

"Vanilla?"

Someone answered Martha's question. "Yes, those clothes came from B62. Lorraine is a vanilla drinker."

"You said vanilla?"

"Yes, you see, the real stuff has an alcoholic content. Lorraine's half crocked most of the time."

"Well, that's amazing!" chuckled Martha. And so it went. Stuck zippers, missing buttons, underarm stains, paint-stained pants, fish scales in pockets, smelly stuff and then every once in a while,

"Wow, a Patagonia ™ jacket!"

"What's a Patagonia?"

"It's a brand, expensive! I got dibs on that one!"

The group worked many hours; tiresome, not all fun, but they persisted. Then, the day of the sale. Cars pouring into the park and rain pouring down in buckets. The Rec Hall was already flooding. Some things were floating. The outdoor stuff was drenched, but it went on until the last shopping bag crammed full of the dregs went out the door for fifty cents. Everyone was exhausted, soaked, but happy. They decided to delay the cleanup until the next day. The co-chairmen announced they had taken in $3,482.75, and since the expenses were nominal, it was mostly all profit. The bake sale sponsored by the Ladies Club showed sales of $1,116.50—mostly due to Dorothy's doughnuts, which were the best ever!

It was a lot of work. The major workers retired to the co-chair's unit and prepared to celebrate with all the liquid refreshments available. Sunday morning would be a foggy, foggy time!

# CHAPTER 37

# HALF STAFF

Martha soon discovered she had fallen into the habit of checking out the flag pole as she came in either entrance. If it was fluttering away, it was a great day, no sadness. If it was at half staff, well she knew the people in the park would be churning in their own way, wondering "who?" Was it a current resident? It could be the vanilla lady; it could be Frank; he had cancer. Maybe it was George; no, he was too mean to die. Martha felt bad that thought had crossed her mind. Maybe it was a former resident, long gone.

As curious as anyone else, she drove into the parking lot in front of the Rec Hall and saw there was a notice on the door.

*William Kingswell, former resident of A14, died this day, March 19, 2007. 88 years old from Kankakee, Illinois. Left the park 1999. Memorial to Our Lady of Hope Catholic Church, Kankakee, Illinois. Survived by wife, Susan, four children, eleven grandchildren, and six great grandchildren.*

Those few words summed up a life, a long life; a life well lived Martha thought.

She had heard nothing about William Kingswell. It struck her as rather strange, this passing in and out of strangers. Some left and were gone like ships in the night, silently, leaving nary a ripple. Some departed with a loud bang and left a hole in the park's consciousness when they departed.

She remembered the first funeral she had attended in the Rec Hall Church. The woman's name was Lee. She was a force in the park. She buzzed around in her cart greeting everyone. She kept the church running. She collected dues; she dropped off casseroles to the sick and visited the sad. This woman was a power house of compassion and energy.

Martha had truly liked her and was a little intimidated by her. This was a WOMAN! The funeral was well done and touching. Friends spoke lovingly; the choir sang on key, the minister spoke haltingly with gratitude for her many gifts of time and care to the church and to the community.

This life was celebrated, a life well lived and leaving an empty space behind. Martha wondered at the different impact of so many different lives on the "life of the park." And then life went on as it had for more than thirty-five years. She thought of the many who had preceded her and she felt a sense of gratitude toward them.

They had built the framework on which all would come later. She was continuing in their foot steps. The thought gave her pause. It was truly a living, continually evolving, changing being, and she now knew she was part of it.

She was warmed, too, by the care and attention to protocol the flag people evidenced. The World War II/Korean Veterans were fewer and fewer as the years passed. The American Legion and VFW members kept the procedure going as it should be and they were proud to do so. Patriotism, respect for those who had served was perhaps not as strong as it had been before. An unpopular war can do that. But people were remembered with devotion. This was one of the strengths of the residents of Live Oaks Mobile Home Park. Martha was more than a little proud of the entire process.

# CHAPTER 38

# THE PICNIC

One of the last events in the park was the annual picnic. It was designed to be, Martha discovered, a thank you to the residents who had planned and supported the many Booster activities of the season. It was to be low in cost, five dollars each, and included hamburgers with all the trimmings, potato salad, ice cream bars. The park manager provided the beer and the soda.

There were countless games of skill. Three-wheel bike agility routes, balloon busting, bean bag toss, horse shoes, shuffle board, pitching, putting, basket ball free throw shooting, and many more. A parade of decorated bikes and golf carts preceded the festivities led by costumed walkers. It was quite a sight. Everyone seemed to be in a fun mood.

The weather was warm and sunny. The competition was fierce, but good natured. Most importantly, there was a band. Some CDs accompanied by good singers. People danced; "YMCA" was a winner. Happiness flooded the faces.

It was a time close to the final goodbyes. Some found the goodbyes difficult. More than a few had tears in their eyes. They were all aware of the fragile nature of their time together. Perhaps that is why the people lingered. Of course, the keg of beer was not yet emptied!

Prizes were awarded; free passes were given out for the next season's events. The shuffle board games took forever to finish, and Joe threw out his arm pitching the horse shoes. No one else was injured. No one fell off the three wheelers or bounced off the balloons they were trying to break. Water balloons were tossed here and there. Only one lady, Sarah, was ticked off because she had had her hair set just for the event.

So it was over, another landmark event – ninety percent turnout, everything eaten. The watermelon seed spitting contest hit a record. The Uncle Sam costume won the costume event. The Brittany Spear costume was well received by only a few. A good day. Fun in the sun. Laughter, good food, excellent music. Aren't we the lucky folks! Martha went home smiling.

# CHAPTER 39

## BETH'S VISIT

Beth was due tomorrow.  Martha was eagerly antic-
ipating the visit.  There had been many late night conversa-
tions, some tearful, some hysterically funny, as they shared
life's craziness.  She was aware that something new and different was taking place in Beth's life, but she wasn't sure
what it might be.  Certainly the burden of friendship had
cast a heavier load on Beth's shoulders these last few years
than on hers.  Beth was to arrive by herself, did not need to
be picked up, and was driving a new car.

An hour or so later, a car slowly drove up and
stopped in front of Martha's unit.  A cute little Honda con-
vertible.  Beth was driving, but a tall white-haired man was
sitting next to her, and smiling at her.  Wow!  That was a
new wrinkle!  Out they came and up the steps, and Martha
was introduced to Ben.  She offered her hand after hugging
Beth and he grabbed her in a bear-like hug and said how
excited he was to meet someone who shared Beth's heart.

While a bit put off by the change in her friend's cir-
cumstances, she liked him immediately.  He was warm,
genuine, and he obviously cared deeply for Beth.  They
touched, their eyes met, they laughed together.  It was a
lovely thing to see and Martha was truly thrilled.  Beth had
been her rock for these many years.  She had found someone and they were great together.

So plans were made; lunch was rollickingly successful.  Ben was funny in the kindest way possible, and a joy

to have around.  They toured the area as a threesome and Martha was OK with that.  They ate out, went to the beach, biked around, and swam in the pool, always moving and always in high spirits.

Martha had arranged for a day fishing trip for Ben with some of the guys in the park.  After he had boarded the boat crammed full with fishing gear, sandwiches and beer, she and Beth took off on their own.  She needed to talk and Beth sensed the need, as she had always been able to do.

# CHAPTER 40

## BETH'S VISIT, PART II

"Okay, Martha, what's up? You're brimming over with something. What's on your mind? It's got to be important to you."

"It is and I can't seem to put it all into words."

"Give it a try."

"All right. Well, compared to China, we as a country haven't even been weaned."

"China, weaned? Where are you going with this?"

"The subject is AGE. We don't know how to deal with it. Our country doesn't. I don't know how. The people here try, but we truly haven't the slightest idea how to go about it."

"Wow, that's heavy. Tell me more."

"Well, we had roles to play. We had lines to read; we had costumes to wear; we were at home with the scenery of our lives, and now, we're still on life's stage, and we have no lines, no role to play, no purpose. We're not vital anymore!"

"You're really into this aren't you?"

"Yes, it drives me nuts. I feel like I'm part of the planned obsolescence program in our society. Ready to be trashed and it irritates the hell out of me!"

"I can see that," said Beth, "or I think I see. What do you want to do about it? How can I help?"

"I don't know the answer to either question. You see, I'm not ready for the trash compactor. I'd like to climb up

Machu Pichu, and my legs couldn't make it, and I don't have the money to get there."

"In Peru?"

"Yes, in Peru. I'd like to scuba dive along the Barrier Reef in Australia, and my lungs wouldn't be strong enough, and it costs too much to get there, too. I'd like to run up and down the Halls of Congress and bang their heads together, yell at them to stop trashing the President, each other, posturing – both sides and get on with it."

"My, my," said Beth. "You are really worked up about all of this. So, where are you going with this?"

"Nowhere, I guess. It's just that I want to feel vital. I want to have a role to play, and I don't know what it is. I've been a daughter, a lover, a wife, a mother, a dedicated professional, a good friend, a pot luck organizer, a golfer, a swimmer, and that's not enough, and Time's running out. Pretty soon my stuff will be on the curb, and I'll be gone, and never know what I might have become! I dream of mind blowing sex, and guess what? I don't even have a vibrator!"

"Oh, Martha, you're sticking pins in yourself for no reason. This is self-induced pity. Our roles change certainly, but you've never been without purpose, without being vital."

"Is that right? Why don't I think so?"

"You can help usher your granddaughter through the intimidating jungle of high school. You can cushion the impact of menopause on your daughter, Pam. You give moral encouragement to Bill Jr. as he starts his own business. Yes, you can always be there for him. You co-chair pot lucks and chili dinners, and drive your almost blind friend to Publix. Those are vital activities."

"In retrospect, Beth, they don't seem to be."

"Well, they are. You are vital. Vital to me and countless others. It's just a different kind of vitality. Buy a snorkel and snorkel in the pool; rent a llama; get a fish tank. Hey, you can do it, kiddo. I'll buy you a vibrator, and one of those German things!"

"Thank you, dear person; I had to get those things out. I'm really pretty good. The anger of those hopeless years when Bill drifted away still haunts me. Thanks for listening."

"I'm always happy to do that; you know that, Martha."

"Yes, I do. Friends forever. I'm really happy you and Ben found each other."

"Well, I sure am! Yes, Friends forever."

# CHAPTER 41

## THE "MUST GO" PARTY

The end of the season was drawing near. Martha was scanning the headlines in the local paper. She smiled to herself realizing how unfamiliar she had been with the names of towns and cities just a few months ago. She didn't feel like a native "cracker," but she didn't consider herself a complete outlander either. She had been talking to one of her newer friends, Mae, about putting together a "must go" party as the snow birds—and she was one—were looking at their fridges and freezers in dismay, knowing they were soon to leave. A generation that had survived the depression and war years tended to over buy when they saw the plenty available so close at hand. The idea was to bring together all the extra food and have a final bash. Most of the food couldn't be taken to the help centers, so why not have a fun time together and use up the leftovers? Mae was highly enthusiastic, so the plans were taking shape.

Martha had suggested that those who were willing donate a vase—everyone had a few extra flower vases around. Everyone's kids sent flowers when they didn't know what else to send. Then she would put a tea light in the bottom and decorate the tables with them.

The day of the event arrived. Mae had to run out for more tea lights, vigil lights as more than one hundred vases arrived. That was pretty amazing. One hundred and thirty six people had signed up and since they had no idea what would be arriving, and in what quantity, it was a shaky two-some who greeted the arrivals. They were overwhelmed with what came in. There were twenty pies, half still frozen, eight large meat loaves, six pots of sausage and sauerkraut, twelve cakes, one hundred and forty cupcakes, fifteen quarts of ice cream, twenty-five chicken casseroles, ten bowls of baked beans, biscuits, bread, rolls, thirty-two bottles of catsup, eighteen mustards, fourteen relishes, and on and on! They were a little short on salads, but no matter.

The tables looked great, the tea lights were blinking, and people were roaming around visiting and enjoying the time together. It was such a good feeling as everyone there knew that some might not be back in the fall, which made this time more precious.

Martha and Mae were beaming and then someone grabbed Martha's arm.

"Mrs. Jenkins?"

"Yes, call me Martha."

"I'm Doris Henley. Where are my yams? I don't see them."

"Your yams?"

"Yes, are you hard of hearing?"

"No, not really. What yams?"

"The bowl I brought; there were flowers on the edges and it was a new recipe and I wanted to taste them."

"Oh, Mrs. Henley was it?"

"Yes."

"Well, you see …"

At that point Martha looked at Mae for help and Mae disappeared into the kitchen.

"I remember the bowl. Whatever was in it was frozen and there was a green hue on top, and no name. So we didn't put it out. It's back in the kitchen if you want to get it."

"Well, I never!" And with that Mrs. Henley stalked out.

Mae reappeared and was holding her hands over her face trying not to laugh.

"That lady always brings stuff to the pot lucks she's had in her freezer for years, and we always leave it in the kitchen. I didn't see it or I would have warned you. Don't worry; everything is going great. There's plenty of food and everyone is having fun. The vases were a great idea. Come on; let's eat!"

A while later, they looked around the hall and smiled.

"OK, Mae, I feel like I was hit by a truck. It was good, right?"

"It was good!"

And arm in arm they headed into the kitchen, a pile of dishes and pots and pans awaited.

# CHAPTER 42

## OHIO BOUND

April 7th arrived. She wanted to be home by Easter. Even though her grandkids were getting older, they still enjoyed an Easter Egg Hunt. Pam and Beth had both offered to fly down and drive back with her, but she had thankfully said no. She wanted to do this by herself—close up, do all the countless things she had to do.

The list was pretty amazing: Saran Wrap ™ on the toilet seat, put Damp Rid™ under the bed, vinegar in the drains. Well, she was ready. She had said her goodbyes, left a little gift for Paul and Betty Tyler. She could never truly thank them enough for all their many kindnesses. As she drove out the entrance, she saw Ernie sitting on his three wheeler; he saluted and said,

"Goodbye, Missus. See you in October. You drive with care now. I'll be checking on your place, no worry." And he saluted.

"Goodbye, Ernie." And she returned the salute.

Her thoughts were a mixed bag of so many things. She realized that she had made a home there. She had friends; she felt part of that community. It was a strange feeling. So many different life stories, so many different places of origin, occupations, life styles, and yet in some bizarre way they seemed to function as a group. When there was need, they responded. She remembered the sad eyes she had seen her first time in the Rec Hall. She had tried to seek them out. Some had responded; some were aloof and closed, but almost every single person was kind. As time passed, she realized she had not hidden her sadness as she had before.

She felt she had been given a new life, a gift of community and commitment, and she was grateful. She would return to Live Oaks Mobile Home Park in the fall. Somehow she sensed she was a more complete person than when she had arrived in January, and this was truly a gift. So, she was driving the road north, singing with the radio, and not so alone anymore.

The road ahead was open, the traffic light, the sun shining. She was going home to what? She wasn't at all sure. What she did know, and was certain of was that she had just left a home, and she would return.

As a golden oldie filled the car with familiar sounds, a thought popped in her mind. "Why don't I write a book about all I've experienced here at Live Oaks Mobile Home Park?" Why not?

# ON AGEING

When you see me sitting quietly,
Like a sack left on the shelf.
Don't think I need your chattering,
I'm listening to myself,
Hold!  Stop!  Don't pity me!
Hold! Stop! Your sympathy!
Understanding if you've got it
Otherwise I'll do without it!

When my bones are stiff and aching,
And my feet won't climb the stair
I will only ask one favor
Don't bring me no rocking chair.

When you see me walking, stumbling,
Don't study and get it wrong.
'Cause tired don't mean lazy
And every goodbye ain't gone
I'm the same person I was back then
A little less hair, a little less chin
A lot less lungs and much less wind.
But ain't I lucky I can still breathe in.

Written by Maya Angelou,
published by Peter Bedrick Books

## Martha's Mobile Home Park

**But it is also Peg Grimm's Home**

**Peg can be reached at placidapeg@yahoo.com**

# About the Author Peg Grimm

Encapsulate 83 years of living? One might mention her jumping from a second floor balcony with an umbrella at age 8. Perhaps one might recall her nearly drowning, coming to believing she was in heaven and not at all happy at age 13.

One might reflect on her 56 year marriage where she discovered the passion and the kindness of love. Should we suggest the pride in her two daughters or the joy she found in teaching? She would include the value of friends who brought light and color to her dark and sunny days; and, of course, her delight in forming words and phrases.

Obviously we must consider her constant belief in the goodness of humankind. Above all else, we should report her unbridled sense of humor, her need for laughter, and her love of life itself.

Printed in the United States
205402BV00002B/235-486/P